MY SON IS A MURDERER

Written by Spencer Guerrero

Copyright © 2023 by Spencer Guerrero

All rights reserved.

No portion of this book may be reproduced in any form without written permission from the publisher or author, except as permitted by U.S. copyright law.

This is a work of fiction. All characters, names, places, and events are the product of the author's imagination or used fictitiously.

Contents

Trigger Warning — V

1. PROLOGUE — 1
2. CHAPTER 1 — 3
3. CHAPTER 2 — 10
4. CHAPTER 3 — 24
5. CHAPTER 4 — 34
6. CHAPTER 5 — 46
7. CHAPTER 6 — 60
8. CHAPTER 7 — 72
9. CHAPTER 8 — 85
10. CHAPTER 9 — 102
11. CHAPTER 10 — 114
12. CHAPTER 11 — 123
13. CHAPTER 12 — 140
14. CHAPTER 13 — 150
15. CHAPTER 14 — 160

16.	CHAPTER 15	178
17.	CHAPTER 16	190
18.	CHAPTER 17	198
19.	CHAPTER 18	221
20.	CHAPTER 19	228
21.	CHAPTER 20	236
22.	CHAPTER 21	240
23.	EPILOGUE	258
24.	THE END.	263
25.	THANK YOU READER!	264
26.	PLEASE REVIEW!	265
27.	MORE BOOKS AVAILABLE!	266
28.	DEDICATION	267
29.	ABOUT THE AUTHOR	269

Trigger Warning

POTENTIAL SPOILERS BELOW

This book includes murder, death, domestic abuse, mental abuse, suicide, sexual harassment, mention of sexual assault, mention of pe-

dophilia, non-graphic mentions of CP, and some intense scenes of violence.

Reader Discretion Is Advised.

PROLOGUE

Henry Cain was a high school student and a popular star athlete. He measured six-foot-two and weighed one-hundred-ninety pounds. He had curly blonde hair and sea-green eyes. He was also dead. He was messing with people he shouldn't have, and he let out a dark secret. It pushed everything over the edge. He should've never walked through the Blackwood Forest that day. It changed his fate forever. It was a mile west of Skyview High. While his classmates would continue to attend class, eat lunch, joke around, play sports, and go on with their young lives, Henry's life was tragically over. He was being viciously stabbed, and slashed to death by a sharp blade, ripened with his oozing dark blood. While Henry clutched his split-open throat, blood spilled over his hands like a waterfall, staining his clothes. He choked on his own blood and silently pleaded *why?* Over and over again.

As a final blow, she pushed him over the hillside after the deadly confrontation. Henry let out a blood-gurgling shriek as he dropped fast and hard. He gruesomely landed on his back on top of a large, jagged rock near a flowing ravine. *Crunch.* Henry's spine shattered instantly as his shocked eyes rolled back, and his jaw went slack. Henry's killer peeked over and saw his dead body. At first his killer smirked, satisfied with the outcome. But then reality set in, and a hundred thoughts stormed his mind all at once.

The raging guilt broiled in his stomach causing him to violently puke into the river. Bullets of sweat raced down his forehead, as he climbed down the hill towards the water, to vigorously clean off Henry's blood from his hands.

He took Henry's phone and smashed it to pieces with his foot. The cold-blooded killer then took one long gaze at Henry's lifeless body and sprinted away, leaving it to rot. He charged through the forest like a frightened animal, as his legs burned with agonizing pain. The sharp air tore through his lungs like icicles. He stumbled, and fell— his nerves wracked. He wasn't in the best shape, but he powered through. Sheer adrenaline surged through his veins as he tried to escape the most horrific crime he had ever committed. She stayed behind, to watch. To watch Henry's gruesome corpse.

He glanced down and saw that his shirt was filled with Henry's blood. The bloodied knife was also still in his possession. He quickly pulled off his shirt. He folded the knife and placed it inside his pocket. Both objects were incriminating evidence, but the killer had no intention of ever being caught. He had a plan to frame someone else.

Someone else would take the fall for the grisly murder that shocked the town, and destroyed the Cain family forever. They would never be the same ever again. All because of a dark secret and a shocking lie, that unraveled everything.

CHAPTER 1

As a mother, I'd never believe that my son would be accused of murder. Especially when it came to the murder of his *best friend*. It didn't make any sense to me. I raised Ethan, and I *knew* that deep down he was a good kid. Was I really capable of raising a murderer?

It happened after school, in the Blackwood Forest. I was a high school teacher myself, and I taught English. I had many interactions with kids that were my son's age. He was like them. He was normal, and kind. You needed to be a different kind of person to slash someone's neck over and over and over again while they begged for mercy. You needed to have hate and rage in your heart. You needed to have a soul that was lost. Those were the things I told myself anyway. I was determined to think anything to convince myself that my son was not capable of committing a brutal, gruesome murder. I didn't care what anyone had to say. Ethan was not a killer. All I could think of when I heard that Ethan was accused of Henry's murder was that *we all lie to save ourselves*. Someone out there was lying— covering their own part in Henry's murder.

The sooner I accepted that, the sooner I could find the truth behind his tragic death.

BEFORE

I imagined my life before the nightmare that consumed our lives. On a regular morning, I would cook breakfast for Ethan and his younger brother, Santiago. We called him *Santi*. Two eggs with cheese, no onions and two strips of bacon with two pancakes drizzled with maple syrup. That was their favorite. One time I made the eggs with onions, and it turned into world war three in my house.

Skyview was a decent enough town. The worst things were the occasional violent drug busts, and teenagers blasting profanity-laced music in public. Some of Ethan's teammates on the basketball team loved that type of music, especially Henry.

We made ourselves at home in a modest, two-story house with a small-ish backyard. It had three rooms and two bathrooms. I couldn't ask for more, especially on a teacher salary. Santi was patiently seated at the dining table while Ethan was still dragging himself out of bed. That was usually how that went.

I had silky brown hair that hung around my shoulders, olive skin and warm brown eyes. I usually wore grey pantsuits with black flats and a silver necklace. I liked to keep it simple.

Santi took after me with his brown, curly mop-top of hair and coffee-colored skin. He had bright, brown eyes which reflected his curiosity and love of studying. He was thin and short and as a result didn't play any sports. Ethan on the other hand was lanky, athletic, and always had a skin fade with his pitch-black, straight hair. He soared through the air like Michael Jordan when he played. Those were his words, not mine. He had dark, baggy eyes and a charming, gap-toothed smile. He used that smile to win over Layla Forrester's heart.

"How's the breakfast, sweetheart?" I asked.

"It's super delicious. You make the best breakfast ever, mom," Santi said with a mouthful.

I smiled to myself. I was happy he wasn't going through his coming-of-age stage yet. I didn't love that part of raising kids. The part where they hate you and they hate the world even more. Ethan was smack in the middle of his, but he was better than most.

"You make the best breakfast ever mommy!" Ethan mocked as he strode in and bopped Santi on the head.

"Hey! Stop it."

"Don't mock your brother. He's telling the truth," I said.

"Yeah, yeah, yeah. Can I have your pancake?" Ethan asked Santi as he sat down.

"I want it."

"I want it more. I'm your big brother so you have to listen to me."

"Okay, fine. I'll wait for mom to make more," Santi replied.

"Sweet."

"Ethan, if you take that I will bite off your hand," I warned.

"But he said I could take it," Ethan pleaded.

"Don't do that to him."

Ethan knew that Santi looked up to him and even admired him. It's what little brothers did to big brothers. Especially since the dad wasn't around much.

"Alright, fine. I'll be nice."

"I can eat it?" Santi asked.

"All yours, little man."

Santi began to engulf his food as I served Ethan, minutes later.

"Still in pajamas? Really?"

"Layla has my clothes in her car."

"And why is that?" I asked.

"Do I really have to say it? I don't think anyone at this table wants to hear it."

"Nope. We had the talk. I'm good."

"What talk?" Santi asked.

I glared at Ethan and quietly dared him to confess.

"Uh, nothing. Layla and I have fashion shows in her car. She's into that stuff."

"Do you guys get naked? Ew!" Santi shrieked.

"I have no comment."

I mixed together my coffee with hot water and creamer and sat down next to my sons. It was hard having kids, but I would do anything for them, and I lived for moments like that. When we all got to be together.

"How's school, Santi?" I asked.

"Good! I have high grades in Geometry, Chemistry, English, World History and in my robotics class. I built a robot hand that can grab objects. We used it on a mango!" Santi exclaimed.

"A mango? That's awesome."

"Wow, a whole mango? Holy shit, dude! You're gonna change the world," Ethan teased.

"Yeah, I am gonna change the world. Smart ass," Santi snapped.

I gasped and gaped at Santi as he giggled. We all warmly laughed as we enjoyed each other's company.

"How about you, Ethan?" I asked.

"It's whatever. I've had basketball practice all week. The practices are ending later than usual. I need to beat out Henry for a starting spot. Dude really thinks he's better than me."

"Why do you have to beat him? Can't you both start or something?"

"You don't get it, mom."

"Can you explain then?"

"We play the same position. We're both small forwards. I've told you this."

"Well, I forgot. I'm not a basketball star am I?"

"Whatever, mom," Ethan shook his head.

"You know I'm right."

"You're a star at being a mom."

"Thank you, Santi. That's sweet," I smiled.

Ethan's face was permanently glued to his phone as his thumbs tapped away at the screen.

"Do you really need to text Layla every second of every day?"

"She needs reassurance. She'll die without me."

"Reassurance of what?"

"That I still love her and that I will continue to love her forever," Ethan smiled.

"You're kidding, right?"

"Yes mom. She's outside. I gotta go, bye!" Ethan sprang up, bopped Santi, and kissed my head as he flew out the front door. I shook my head at Santi.

"Promise me, you won't be like that when you get a girlfriend."

"I promise mom."

"I don't think I believe you."

"I don't believe me either. Girlfriends are awesome," Santi giggled.

"He doesn't even take a backpack."

"Only his duffel bag. He's a delinquent,"

"I'm surprised you know what that word means," I chuckled.

"I'm not your average thirteen-year-old. I know things."

"You are definitely not average."

"That's why dad wants me to work on the *force*."

A knot formed in my stomach. Any time their father suggested them to do anything, I wanted to strangle him. He had no place after what he did to me and to them.

"Well, do you want to be a cop?" I swallowed hard. I had to try my best to hide my disdain. I didn't want to completely influence my son's decisions even if I disapproved of them. They needed to make good choices for themselves.

"Nah, not really."

"Then maybe you shouldn't be a cop. Do something that you like, my child."

"Do you think he'll talk to me more if I become a cop?"

The knot grew tighter, and my eyes turned misty. I hated hearing things like that. Why did a son have to win over his own father's attention? It reminded me of my own father. That was the worst part.

"I don't know, Santi. I would say probably not. He's your dad. He should be talking to you more because you're his son. There's no other reason or condition needed."

"Do you think things would be better if you had not divorced?"

"I explained to you why we had to, Santi."

"It's not fair. I don't like it."

"He caused me a lot of pain, son. You'll understand when you're older."

"You say that every year."

"I'll keep saying it until you understand."

"We're gonna be late."

One day you'll understand why I hate your father with a burning passion, I thought.

CHAPTER 2

Nestled amidst neatly manicured lawns and tree-lined streets, Skyview High stood smack in the middle of our town, Skyview Falls. The Campus was expansive, as it had multiple buildings interconnected by sidewalks and hallways. The entrance was marked by a showy sign and banner that displayed the school's name and motto.

No goal's too high where Skyhawks fly.

The school's mascot was actually changed to the Suns, but they didn't know how to make a new motto that rhymed so they never bothered to change it. It was above my paygrade to think of a new one.

In the middle of the school was the main building that housed administrative offices, the auditorium, and most classrooms. It was a three-story tower with large windows that invited natural light and offered glimpses of what was happening inside. Some of it would be learning and most of it would be students goofing off.

The school had a lively atmosphere during the day, with students bustling between classes, chit-chatting, and taking selfies for their Instagram stories. The main hallway had bulletin boards and display cases that showed upcoming events, sports trophies, and other student achievements. The Skyview Suns basketball team had more achievements than any other sports club. There was a history of champions there and a long, storied legacy that would eventually be tarnished forever.

As I click-clacked to my classroom, I greeted colleagues and students I liked and didn't like. There was one teacher I particularly didn't care for, Mr. Griffin. He was the hunched-over, pornstache-sporting history teacher who desperately held onto the six strands of hair he had on his mostly bald scalp. He always wore his dress pants too tight, and he smelled like mayonnaise. It wasn't just his appearance and style choices. Mr. Griffin had a *reputation*. He used to be the baseball coach, but then something happened, and he got removed. We all heard the whisperings, but it was never confirmed. I chose not to investigate any further and simply avoided him. I focused on my work. Students made up nasty rumors all the time about teachers. We never knew if we could believe them.

I made sure to breathe through my mouth as I passed him standing outside his class.

"Hey Ms. Salvador. I love your heels. They sound powerful!" Mr. Griffin roared.

"Thank you, Mr. Griffin. Have a good day," I replied as I picked up the pace.

I had no intention of starting a conversation with that foul, suspicious man. It wasn't a crime to be weird, but I still had an odd feeling about him. There was something off about him. He tried too hard to be nice. I thought I was being cruel until I later learned the truth about him. I turned the final corner to get to my classroom and saw my beloved son devouring Layla's face. I cringed yet bravely marched forward.

"Really? This early?" I asked.

Ethan and Layla quickly detached from each other and tried to act like nothing had happened.

"Why are you stalking me?" Ethan asked.

"I'm not stalking you. My classroom is right there."

He turned around and nodded.

"Oh, yeah. That's right."

"I'm sorry, Ms. Salvador. We meant no disrespect," Layla urged.

"It's okay, Layla. You were having your breakfast. I understand."

"You're not funny, mom."

Layla was a petite, athletic girl with short brown curls and piercing blue eyes. She had cocoa-colored skin and was the best girlfriend my son ever had. She was kind-hearted and was into sports like him. She ran track. I only hoped her strict studying habits would rub off on him eventually.

"I'm still sorry, Ms. Salvador. I shouldn't be kissing your son in front of your classroom."

"Layla, you can call me Sonya. Did you do the reading assignment I uploaded last night?" I asked.

"Yes ma'am. I finished it first thing."

"What an excellent student. Why can't you be like her, Ethan?"

"You compare me to my brother, and you compare me to my girlfriend. Who's next, my dad?"

"You're nothing like your father."

"If you say so."

"*You're not,*" I said forcefully.

Layla awkwardly stayed silent while she rubbed my son's back.

"I'm gonna go inside the room," Layla said as she rushed inside as the bell rang.

"You should get to class. You're late," I suggested.

"I know," Ethan stomped away.

I didn't know what had gotten into him lately, but I could only assume it had to do with his father. If Santi expressed having issues with him, odds were Ethan had similar feelings. I absolutely hated him for making my children feel that way.

As I waltzed into my classroom, I had to set aside those feelings of silent rage and put on a happy face for my students. It wasn't hard as I had tried my best to make my classroom not look like a prison cell. While the rest of the school's rooms resembled ice-cold, solitary confinement cells, I wanted to add some color to my own room. Each of my four walls were decorated with educational posters which showcased inspirational quotes, vibrant art pieces, and displays of exemplary student work. In one corner, I had a cozy rug with a large wooden bookshelf filled to the brim with books that were necessary for the passing of my class. I tried my hardest to make my students excited. I knew they thought school was boring beyond belief. I would be lying if I said I didn't feel that way sometimes as well.

I loved teaching once, but as time went on I just tried to survive. I felt trapped with no way out. But, I had always been a survivor.

I was forced to. I had to take care of myself and take care of my sons. I couldn't allow myself to wallow in self-pity. That was the road to destruction. That was the road to damaging my children's souls. They had enough trauma from their father.

My classroom was always buzzing with lively laughter and chatter. They only hushed when I whacked my ruler against my desk to indicate silence. The only one who kept talking was Henry Cain. It wasn't a surprise to me. He had a wide frame and a block of a head. My son joked that he looked like a Lego character. The only reason I tolerated his tomfoolery was because he was Ethan's best friend, but he was getting worse as the year went on.

"Okay class, good morning. I hope everyone had a good breakfast and a good night's sleep. I can see that the front row is half-dead. That's a good sign."

My students giggled as they took out their notebooks and pencils. Layla already had everything out, neatly organized on her desk. Henry sat beside her and whispered to her. She looked annoyed and rolled her eyes on occasion.

"Today we're gonna be discussing last night's online assignment. I gave you a passage to read from Shakespeare and we're gonna learn how he wrote drama so effectively," I said as I glared at Henry for continuing to talk.

"I see you looking at me, Sonya. Don't fall in love," Henry teased.

The class laughed as I kept my cool.

"Please address me as Ms. Salvador, Henry. I treat you with respect, please return the courtesy."

"I didn't mean to offend you. I'll gladly treat you with respect. Just give me the chance. I know you're single."

The entire class laughed. Layla shook her head, disapproving of his antics.

Has this kid lost his mind? I thought.

"Henry, do you want to go to indoor suspension for this period?" I asked.

"Only if it means I get to see you after school to make up the work."

The entire class was *oooooing*. He was crossing a line.

"You're on very thin ice right now, Henry. You're wasting my time and the class's time with your rude comments."

"Don't worry, I'll tell Ethan not to wait up for you since you'll be busy with me."

"You're getting written up," I said as I furiously opened my desk drawer, yanked out a pink slip and jotted down my reasoning to get Henry the hell out of my class. He slung his backpack over his shoulder and slid over to my desk. I handed him the pink slip and pointed towards the door.

"Goodbye Henry. Please behave yourself next time."

"Trust me, I know how to behave."

"The door is that way."

"Pink? My favorite color," Henry laughed as he softly grabbed it and walked out with an obnoxious smirk on his face. Before he left he pointed at Layla and winked at her. She waved him off.

"Get out now!" I commanded.

"Okay, okay. Don't get all *yelly*.".

"You forced me to be *yelly*."

"Don't tease me with a good time, Ms. Salvador," Henry grinned as he ran down the hall.

I really wanted to give him a piece of my mind, but he was Ethan's best friend and for his sake, I wouldn't cause a scene in front of everyone. Especially since Layla was there. She almost looked afraid. I wondered what the hell Henry was whispering to her. I attempted to get the class back on track to continue with my lesson.

I usually ate lunch alone. I didn't get along with the other English teachers. They were well into their 50s and 60s. I just felt out of place, and it was hard for me to have a conversation with them after they heard about what had happened between me and Felix. I hated the way they looked at me. It was a mixture of shame and pity. They asked me so many burning questions about how it happened, and they made it seem like it had been my fault. Maybe it partly was, to a degree, but I didn't feel like spilling every last personal detail of my life to them. They always gossiped with each other and to their students. I didn't need that in my life. Not after everything I had been through.

I liked to eat on a stone bench underneath the shade of a palm tree. It was far away from the main courtyard where the student body ate. I didn't like being there. I heard and saw things that made my stomach twirl.

Would you have sex with a monkey?

I have this rash on my butt. Wanna see?

Dude I got so drunk I almost crashed my dad's Tesla into a brick wall.

I'm done with girls. I'm convinced they're all psychos. That's the last time Alison licks me there.

If he breaks up with me, I swear I'll like die. He's literally my one and only.

Those are just a few of the snippets I've heard throughout the years. It was mildly entertaining for a while, but I wanted to keep my distance. High school students as I realized were capable of many, many things that included bullying, cruelty, and murder. I sometimes ate with my best friend, Willow Jacobson. She was the high school principal. Everyone knew we were close, so I usually got the side-eye. We had been best friends since before she became the principal so I paid no mind to the *haters*, as my kids would say. Willow was busy that day so no girl time. It was a good thing though, or else I might've not seen them.

When I was done eating, I threw everything away in the trash and prepared myself to get back to my classroom. I entered the main hallway that connected the buildings to the courtyard and took the long trek back. I stopped dead in my tracks when I passed Henry and Layla. They were close together. At first glance, I thought the worst.

Is Layla cheating on my son with his best friend?

But no, it wasn't that. Henry was pinning Layla's arms against a wall, in a corner that was hidden from many angles. You had to be right next to them to see them.

"What are you gonna do about it, huh?" Henry asked.

"Please let go of me," Layla pleaded.

"C'mon, try to get out of it."

"Do you want me to tell Ethan about this?"

"He's literally my brother from another mother. He won't care. We're just messing around. C'mon, don't be a buzzkill like Beth."

"Beth isn't a buzzkill. You're just being weird, and she's the principal's daughter," Layla shot back.

"Like I give a shit." Henry giggled.

"Hey! Get your hands off of her right now. We do not touch other students like that," I commanded.

Henry saw me and rocketed his hands into the air.

"Oh no, the warden's here. Sorry Layla, fun's over."

"It didn't look like she was having fun."

"Yeah well, you just got here. You didn't see much. You shouldn't assume things."

"Care to explain what I didn't see?" I dared.

"Nah, that's between Layla and I."

"Layla, are you okay? What did he do to you?" I asked, my voice rising.

The amount of fury I felt was coursing through my veins like fire. My heart was thumping so loud, I heard every beat in my ears.

"No, nothing, Ms. Salvador. It's fine. Nothing happened."

"See? The lady says nothing happened. You're getting worked up over nothing."

"You still had your hands on her, and you will be reported for that."

"You're gonna report your son's best friend?" Henry asked.

"Best friends don't touch each other's girlfriends like that."

Henry sighed and hung his head.

"Alright, fine. You're right. I'm sorry. I'm sorry, Layla. I got carried away. I like to goof off, okay? Ethan knows that. I meant no harm. I was feeling antsy during that indoor suspension. They don't let you talk or even scratch your ass. I needed to let loose."

I stayed quiet while I contemplated what to say.

"You could let loose by yourself in a closet."

"Okay then. I guess."

"Are you sure you're okay, Layla?" I asked.

"Yeah, I'm okay. I swear."

"Okay, Henry. I'm still reporting you to the principal because I don't want this sort of thing to happen again. I'm sorry but you caused this. Rules are rules."

"They need me on the basketball team. You can't do this to me. I'm one of the starters."

"I don't care who you are. You're not exempt from the consequences of your actions."

"Whatever. I'll be fine."

"You can go to class."

Henry gave a sarcastic grin and slowly walked away. I got closer to Layla and hugged her.

"You can't let him do that to you, Layla. You should tell Ethan what happened."

"Okay. I will."

She was such a sweet girl. She needed protection. She was too innocent. After school, I stormed into Willow's office. She was a towering, regal woman with shiny brown hair and big brown eyes. I liked to joke that was secretly English royalty. She had that way of carrying herself like an absolute professional when she needed to.

Everything inside her office screamed corporate murder machine. Bland file cabinets stacked like mountains in all corners of the room, grey walls, dim lighting, no windows, freezing air-conditioning, and a massive hardwood desk flooded with folders, papers, binders, and a wired telephone from the 12th century. She was on the phone when I came in and held up a finger to prevent me from shouting out anything. She made a gagging expression which meant it was someone from the school board that she hated. I took the liberty of sitting down across from her and patiently waited. After several minutes of saying *yes*, *got it* and *I understand*, she hung up.

"Goodness gracious, that man does not stop talking."

"Who was it?"

"Some monkey in a suit on the board. He wouldn't stop talking to me about his wife's wine tasting club," Willow rolled her eyes.

"Sounds interesting."

"I'm happy you think so because I'm invited. I couldn't say no. Do you wanna come with me?"

"Not at all."

"I love you too."

"I wish you good luck at your funeral."

"So, are you here to talk about your trash ex-husband or about the other English teachers being annoying?"

"I want to recommend a 3-day suspension for Henry Cain."

"Jesus Christ, not again. He's still disrupting class?"

"It's worse. I saw him pinning Layla against the wall during lunch. They were alone, Willow. It was really strange and inappropriate."

"Oh my god. Do you think they're—," Willow trailed.

"No, I doubt it. Layla isn't like that, but then again what do I know? This is high school. Kids can be finicky. They can have doubts and temptations. They'll stick it in a keyhole if they're that desperate."

"Henry is Ethan's best friend. There's no way he would do that to him, right?" Willow asked.

"I sure hope not. I mean, I don't think so. Henry is hard to read. He can be really charming at times, but then he turns into this rude, aggressive bully who just doesn't care about hurting people's feelings."

"Sounds like someone we know."

My ex-husband, I thought.

"I think he's bothering Beth as well."

"What? Are you serious? Of course she doesn't tell me anything."

"From what I understand, yes."

"What a mess," Willow mumbled.

"When are you going to notify Henry of his suspension?"

"I'm not suspending him."

"What?"

"I know, Sonya. Please don't get upset. I have to approve that with the other vice principals, and then Lawrence needs to be notified. It's a whole thing."

"Lawrence? Are you serious? Henry's father?"

"He donates a lot of money to the school, Sonya. He's an honorary member of the school board. Plus, Henry is a basketball star or whatever. My hands are tied. I can suggest it, but they're gonna find a way to toss it aside. Lawrence always gets what he wants."

"I'm sorry Willow, but that's horseshit. How can you let that happen?"

"You don't think I've tried to get past them before? Be realistic. He has money and power. Our morals and sense of ethics don't matter in this case. He's gonna win every time."

"I refuse to believe that."

"I don't know what else to say. It pisses me off, but it's a battle not worth fighting because we can't win it. Trust me, Beth is apparently involved so I am pretty enraged."

"Henry needs to be taught a lesson. No wonder he acts the way he does. He knows he can get away with it. He's a privileged little shit."

"Welcome to my world, Sonya."

"That's ridiculous, that's an abuse of power."

"I'm surprised you didn't know Lawrence was on the school board."

"I haven't kept up with those people in a very long time, Willow. I've blocked them out ever since the divorce."

"Maybe if I block Lawrence from my mind he'll stop calling."

"With your luck, he'll call more."

"Screw him. He should call his son and tell him to behave like a regular person."

"Henry will learn soon enough. I believe in karma."

"Hey, I'm sure he will."

"Someone will teach him a real lesson one day. Maybe it'll end up being me."

"Please don't lose your job."

"Maybe I'll teach his mother a lesson too."

"I would pay you thousands of dollars to give Veronica Cain a lesson, in a back alley."

"I'd do it for free."

I should've never said that. I learned later that you had to be careful what you wished for.

CHAPTER 3
PRESENT DAY

It all happened in the blink of an eye, in a white flash of light. One after the other. The beginning of the end. When my world was shattered into a thousand tiny pieces. I was at home, phone on the dining table, sitting alongside Santi. I was helping him with his homework while remaining attentive for Ethan's call. It was almost nine o'clock and I hadn't heard anything from him. He usually came home around six or seven o'clock because his basketball practices ran late. I tried not to freak out and stayed patient. That was around the eighth time he had come home late. Half of me wanted to strangle him when he got home, half of me yearned for him to come home in one piece.

"Are you okay, mom?" Santi asked.

"Yeah, fine. Why?"

"You keep looking at your phone. You're thinking about Ethan, right?"

"You're sure you didn't see or hear anything from him? He didn't tell you he was gonna be home late?"

"Nope. He told me he would see me later and I saw him go into the gym for practice. That was that. It was like normal."

"That's weird, he keeps doing this. Something has to be up."

"Should we ask dad?"

I'd rather drop dead.

"I don't think we need his help yet."

Right on cue, we heard the doorknob being jangled as Ethan tumbled in. He had his warm-up on and was sweating profusely.

"Thank you for calling, Ethan."

"Hello to you too," Ethan said.

"Why are you so sweaty?" I asked.

"I showered but it's a long humid walk from Layla's."

"Is something wrong with your phone?"

"I'm sorry, I ran out of charge. I just saw it. You didn't have to call me thirty-six times, mom."

"I wouldn't have called you so much if you had just answered."

"I'm fine, mom."

"Why have you been coming home so late?"

"I'm at practice and then I go to Layla's," Ethan mumbled.

"Why are the practices running so late now?"

"Are you the curfew Nazi?"

"I am not a Nazi, Ethan. I am your mother. I just want to make sure you're okay."

"You don't need to worry about me. I'm a big boy now."

"Alright, Ethan. That's fine."

"I was with Layla, okay? We were just hanging out after practice. She wanted me to come over because she had my extra clothes and my duffel bag. I was charging my phone there too."

"Can you please send me a text next time?" I asked.

"Mom, you're acting crazy."

"If you say so, Ethan."

Maybe I extended my reach too far, but he was my son. All I wanted to know was if he was safe and sound.

"I'm going upstairs. I need to shower," Ethan slid away.

"Ethan, I'd like to talk about this later."

He ignored me completely. I sighed and sat back down. Santi placed his hand on my arm.

"It's okay, mom."

I grabbed his hand and squeezed.

"I love your brother but sometimes I wanna kill him. He's just being a rebellious teenager, I guess."

"Sometimes I wanna kill him too."

We giggled.

"I'll talk to him before we go to dad's tomorrow."

"Thank you, my love. I just wanna make sure he's okay."

"Me too. You're not crazy, mom."

When it was time for bed, I tried knocking on his door to get him to open.

"Go away!" Ethan shouted.

I chose to let him be and entered my bedroom. It was simple yet elegant. A combination of warm and light brown tones on the walls set the serene atmosphere where I liked to disconnect from the craziness of the real world. Framed pictures of my children were decorated on every wall as well as eccentric artwork which gave the room a sense of personality.

My ex-husband had never allowed me to decorate the room so once we were divorced I took the liberty to do what I wanted. It was the one place where I always felt safe and peaceful. The only place I could truly be alone. A walk-in closet thankfully gave me ample storage for my clothes, shoes, makeup, and skincare products. I didn't have to share anymore either. Another perk from my divorce.

I laid down on my cozy, fluffy bed and tried to go to sleep. I thought about Ethan and the way he had been acting. He was usually better behaved. I chocked it up as him having silly issues with his girlfriend, Layla. He would tell me what was going on eventually. As the night grew late, my eyelids became heavy, and I fell asleep.

I had the nightmare, again. I was at the top of some sort of church or temple watching an older man, dangling off the ledge. Every time I ran towards him to try and save him, he fell off. I watched in horror as his body flew down hard, his anguished screams piercing the air. I never looked away as his body crashed and exploded as it hit the pavement. Dark blood oozed from underneath as bits and pieces of his brain and skull were scattered in his surroundings. His legs were contorted in very unnatural directions and one of his arms had a bloodied bone that penetrated through the skin on his arm.

I always woke up from that nightmare in a cold sweat, trying my best to breathe. I had to muffle my sobbing so my children wouldn't hear. I needed to continue to show them that I was tough and that I was a survivor. I was their rock and their protector. I couldn't and didn't want to rely on their father anymore. I didn't care who he was.

I knew my boys needed me and if I was the only person in the world who had their back, then so be it.

Santi woke me the next morning.

"Good morning, what is it?"

"Dad is here," Santi said.

My heart sank. Every time they left me, it hurt. I hated that he had visitation rights with them. I got dressed, made them breakfast, and walked them to the door. I looked out the peephole and saw a large, rectangular police SUV.

"Why is there a cop car in the driveway?"

"Umm—," Santi trailed.

"He has work. He's gonna drop off us at home."

"Are you kidding me? He's supposed to be spending time with you guys."

"I don't know, mom." Ethan brushed past me and went out the door.

Santi gave me a tight hug and I kissed the top of his head.

"At least one of you still likes me."

"Mom, he's nervous about something. I can tell. He didn't wanna say what, but he's nervous. I think it's a test or basketball or his girlfriend. Sorry I couldn't find out more."

"Oh no, sweetheart. It's okay. Thank you for letting me know. Try to have a good time with your father, make the best of it."

"I'm just gonna catch up on homework. I'll have a lot of time on my hands," Santi sighed.

I affectionately squeezed his shoulder as he ran off and hopped in the car. The police SUV flashed it's bright headlights at me causing me temporary blindness. I wanted to flick him off but remembered that my kids were in the car.

"Asshole," I muttered.

After my kids left, I began grading papers. The one advantage I had with them being with their father was how quiet the house became. Still, I disliked it. I liked hearing them and having them around. It made me happy. It made me feel like I wasn't alone. The hours seemed to stretch on forever as I went through paper after paper. It frustrated me when I saw work that was so abysmal, it was clear the student couldn't care less. There was nothing I could do about that, so I gradually began to accept that most students just cared about sports, video games, doing drugs or chasing girls. I couldn't really fault them. Ethan wasn't too far off.

A sudden ring at the doorbell surprised me. I hadn't ordered any delivery food and I wasn't expecting any packages. I got up and checked the peephole. It was night. I barely noticed it had gotten dark. I groaned. It was Veronica Cain. The woman I hated most. She was a very skinny, elongated Barbie figure with platinum blonde hair and bright blue eyes. She wore ridiculous designer clothing and high heels that made her 9 feet tall. I reluctantly opened the door.

"What do you want, Veronica?"

"Hey Sonya. I'm so sorry to bother you but is my Henry here?"

"No, he's not."

"Shoot. I don't know where he is. He was at practice today and was supposed to walk home but never came. I'm worried sick."

"You could've called. You didn't have to come all the way over here."

"I tried but you blocked me."

"Oh. Well, never mind."

"Will you unblock me?"

"No."

"Okay, fine. That's fair. Are your kids here? Maybe they know where Henry is."

"They're with your Latin lover."

"Right. Well, he's really missing, Sonya. My Henry is missing, and I need to know where he is. If something happened to him, I don't know what I'll do. I know you understand me, mother to mother."

Henry's missing? Oh my god. I wonder if it has something to do with Layla, I thought.

"I'm sorry to hear that. I'm sure he'll turn up, Veronica. You know how kids are."

"Yeah, I'm sure. Thanks anyway. I'll ask Felix to ask Ethan if he's seen Henry."

"You still have Felix's number?"

"Well, yeah. He never blocked me. We still talk about many things. We have a good time," Veronica smirked.

"Goodbye, Veronica," I slammed the door shut.

Every time I finished speaking with Veronica, I was left with a bitter taste in my mouth. She loved to make snarky little comments that dug under your skin. I was curious about Henry and wanted to see how serious it actually was. Veronica was your typical suburban drama queen who loved attention. I couldn't trust her word. I searched up his name and saw that he was already being reported missing on several high school basketball media sites and on local news outlets. I checked social media and saw that his name was trending in the Skyview Falls area. It looked like it was serious after all.

I decided to call Ethan. He had to know something. Santi told me he had been nervous. Could it have been about Henry? Did Ethan know something that no one else knew? Did Henry tell him a secret? Variations of these thoughts revolved around my head as I heard the ring go off for several minutes. After 12 missed calls, I gave up. I was beginning to worry. What the hell was Ethan nervous about? What was going on? I couldn't even drive over to Felix's house because he wouldn't let me in. There'd be a huge fight and I didn't want my boys to see that anymore. They had been through enough.

I went into the kitchen and poured myself a glass of wine. I downed it and went to bed to try and relax. I fell asleep after three straight hours of internally freaking out. It helped a little bit when Santi texted me and told me that Ethan seemed okay. He still wasn't talking, however. I got up for work the next morning and when I strolled into the school I could already tell that things felt different. There was a silence to the school I had never experienced before.

Teachers and students were whispering in the hallways, their faces etched with concern and suspicion. The air was charged, and it felt like something was bound to explode at any minute. My gut twisted onto itself when I saw 4 police officers rushing past me. My curiosity got the best of me, and I quickly followed them.

I needed to know what was going on. I wouldn't have been able to sit still in my classroom without knowing. When they turned a corner, I heard immediate yelling and shouting. My eyes widened in shock when I saw Jonathan Locke grappling with the officers. He struggled against them and tried to yank himself out of their hold. He shouted at them to let him go, which made for a nasty sight. Willow saw what was going on and ushered the spectating students to get to class. She went to my side and threw her hands in the air. We took a few steps back, and cautiously watched the chaotic scene from a distance.

Stop struggling!

We will tase you if you continue!

You're being arrested, stop moving!

These were the things the officers were shouting. Jonathan was a strong, burly basketball player with a massive frame. He had a crew cut and small dark eyes. It was obvious that the officers were nervous. He was a hulking giant that they needed to restrain. One that could easily hurt them.

"Willow why the hell are they doing this in the hallway? There's students around. This is horrifying."

"I tried telling them, but they wanted to take him by surprise. They're taking him into custody."

"Why?"

"They wouldn't tell me."

"Is this related to Henry's disappearance?"

"It has to be."

"Any updates on that?"

"Nope. He's still missing. It's weird, Sonya. It's really weird. No one knows where he went."

Jonathan gave up as he became too tired to fight on. One of the officers placed handcuffs on him and blew out a sigh of relief. They aggressively escorted him out the school as many concerned teachers and students watched.

"It was Ethan! It was Ethan! They hate each other! He had something to do with it! Not me! Let me go! Let me go!" Jonathan shouted.

"Sonya, what the hell?"

"Oh my god," I whispered under my breath.

CHAPTER 4

I was on the verge of tears as I practically sprinted to the class Ethan was supposed to be in. I quickly peeked in through the window in the door and got a lot of confused faces my way. The teacher also looked at me but smiled. I smiled back and staggered away. He wasn't in there. He was supposed to be there. Why wasn't he there? I calmly entered the classroom and excused myself for the interruption.

"Is Ethan Salvador here? He's supposed to be in this class right?" I asked.

"Oh yes but he's absent today. He's your son, isn't he? He's such a delight to teach. Why didn't he come today?" The teacher asked.

My stomach churned with worry as I tried to keep on my best face and not freak the hell out.

"Oh, you know, he was sick. He'll be back tomorrow," I said as I slipped out.

I rushed inside the teacher's bathroom and locked it. Thankfully, Willow was watching my class as I tried to figure out what the hell was going on. I immediately called Layla.

"*Hey Layla, I'm so sorry to bother you but do you know where Ethan is?*" I asked.

"Hey Ms. Salvador. I don't know. He didn't come today. He hasn't answered my calls or texts either so I'm kind of worried. Why didn't he come?"

"I don't know, Layla. I'm not sure. I gotta go, bye," I hung up.

I was officially panicking. Tears poured down my face as my chest tightened. I was hyperventilating as I tried to think of what else to do. I had texted Santi, but he hadn't answered yet. My head pounded as I sent a dozen text messages to Ethan, urging and imploring him to answer. I just needed to hear his voice. That's all I needed. That was the only thing I cared about in the world at that moment. Nothing else mattered to me. After I finally managed to calm myself down, I called Felix. Surprisingly, he answered.

"*What is it Sonya?*" Felix whined.

"*Where the hell is my son, Felix?*" I asked.

"*What's going on? Why do you sound like you've been crying?*"

"*I asked you a god damn question. Where is he?*"

"*Can we relax with the attitude? Jesus, what's going on?*"

"*Ethan isn't here at school. He's absent. You were supposed to take him. Where is he?*"

"*Santi went, but Ethan felt sick, so I let him stay at my house. He's fine. Try not to worry too much. You're freaking me out with the hysterics.*"

"*Henry Cain is missing, Felix. The situation is very urgent.*"

"*I know about Henry. We're all on that and we're gonna find him. Just try to relax please.*"

I hated how nonchalant he was being. It was like he had no idea how it looked. Ethan's best friend was missing, he was absent from school and his teammate, Jonathan Locke was screaming that he had something to do with Henry's disappearance.

"*Why was Jonathan Locke arrested?*"

"*That's part of an ongoing investigation and I can't talk about that. Sorry.*"

"*Why aren't you spending time with your kids? They tell me you don't pay any attention to them.*"

"*Oh my Christ, not this again. I don't have time for this. I work like a dog and when I get home, I need my time to unwind. I don't have the patience to answer Santi's one million questions about random bullshit,*" Felix replied.

He thought his son's desire to speak with his father was random bullshit. I had heard it all.

"*Wow, that's amazing. Are they presenting you with the Father of The Year award at the end of this month or next month?*"

"*I've always hated your sarcasm, you know that?*"

He cursed under his breath and hung up. I couldn't believe I had been in love with him. Once he was charming and sweet. He changed during the marriage, like he couldn't take it anymore. I got pregnant with Ethan at 19 years old and we married soon after. Felix was 24. The first couple of years were great. After that it was very on and off. Especially after Santiago was born. Felix just didn't have what it took to be a dutiful father. I wish I had known that before he planted his seed in me, but I didn't regret it. I loved Ethan and Santi. I had to deal with Felix for the rest of my life, but it was a small price to pay in comparison to my two gifts.

Ethan finally texted me that he was okay, and that he felt very tired. I could finally breathe again. I texted him to please refrain from giving me a massive heart attack. I composed myself and went back to class. Willow was having fun chatting with the students. I walked in with a grin, but the class knew what was going on. They could see the state I was in. They grew quiet the moment I entered. Willow came close to me and held my arm.

"Are you okay? What happened?" Willow asked.

"Ethan is at Felix's place. He was just really tired, so he stayed home. Tough practice I guess."

"Oh, alright. Well, that's great news right?"

"Yeah, of course. Ethan is okay. He's okay."

Willow smiled and walked out.

"Hello class. I'm very sorry for the detour," I announced.

Where's Henry?

Why are your eyes puffy, Ms. Salvador?

Are you okay, Ms. Salvador?

What happened to Henry? Is he really missing?

Why is Henry gone?

Did you see that Jonathan Locke got arrested?

Do you think he killed him or something? Oh my god!

Kids were curious by nature, and they typically said things they shouldn't have said. I couldn't fault them. Henry Cain was their classmate. They wanted to know what had happened to him. I wanted to know too. Soon, we all got our answer.

"I was having a rough day this morning, class. It happens to all of us, but rest assured I'm okay now. As for Henry, I'm not sure where he is. All we can hope is that he turns up and that he's okay. I'm sure he's fine. Maybe he just needed some space for a bit. We're all human. It happens."

They all seemed content enough with that answer, so I began my lesson. I tried my best to focus but the truth was, Ethan and Henry whirled around the back of my mind. It was like I was in the background watching myself teach as questions about them clouded me. That went on for the entire school day until it was finally over. I thanked the heavens and got ready to bolt out of there. Before I left, I saw a crowd forming near the entrance of the basketball gym. Willow was there along with the entire basketball team and Coach Albert. They had flyers in their hands. It had Henry's face on it.

"Alright everyone who wants to go on the search is welcome! We're gonna have multiple police officers, volunteers, and anyone else we can muster searching the Blackwood Forest. The cops think this is where he might've disappeared. He could be hiding in a cave, trapped under a tree, or behind a rock for all we know. One thing's for sure, we will find him, and we will continue to have an amazing basketball season!" Coach Albert bellowed.

The crowd roared and cheered.

"The search is from 3 PM to 9 PM. We need to cover as much ground as possible before dark. The sooner we find Henry, the better the chances are of his survival. We will find him alive and well. I promise you all," Willow announced.

She spotted me in the crowd and pointed at me. I nodded. I wanted to join the search. I called Ethan to see if he would answer and if he wanted to go.

"*Hi mom,*" Ethan said.

"*Why weren't you answering the phone? Are you okay?*"

"*I'm sorry. Are you mad?*"

"*No, it's fine. I was just worried. Are you alright?*" I sighed.

"*Yeah, I was just really tired from practice. Coach Albert worked us hard. That's all.*"

"*Henry was there right?*" I asked.

"*Yeah, he was there. I don't know what's going on mom. He usually walks through the Blackwood to get home, but I guess he never went home.*"

"*What do you think happened?*"

"*I have no idea. Who knows, maybe he's with some girl. Henry's like that. He'll show up. Everyone's gonna kill him when he comes back.*"

It sounded like they were still on good terms. I was confused on what to believe because of what Jonathan Locke said.

"*So you guys are still friends?*"

"*Yeah, why?*"

"*No reason. How well do you get along with Jonathan Locke?*"

"*I don't know. He's cool I guess. He's kind of a giant idiot, but whatever. We need him on the team. He's one of the biggest centers in our district.*"

Maybe Jonathan wasn't telling the truth after all. Maybe he was trying to deflect suspicion. Although that was far from the best way of doing it.

"*Are you joining the search today?*"

"*I'll see. I'm still really sore.*"

"*Ethan, he's your best friend and he's missing.*"

"*I know he is and that's why I'm not worried. I know him better than most. Everyone's freaking out for no reason. That guy is chilling with some college girl in her dorm, and he forgot to charge his phone because he's dumb like that.*"

"*Alright, if you say so. I'll talk to you later. I love you.*"

"*Love you, mom. Bye.*"

I felt a whole lot better going into the search. I reasoned that if Ethan was calm about it, I was going to be calm about it too. Perhaps everyone had allowed Veronica's hysteria to infect them. I couldn't blame her. It was her only son.

As we entered the Blackwood Forest, dozens of footsteps were muffled by a thick layer of fallen leaves, as we urgently marched forward. We were equipped with essential tools and supplies, such as flashlights, walkie-talkies and first aid kits. Many students, teachers, volunteers, and cops aided in the search. Felix was there with Veronica and her husband, Lawrence Whitlock. He was a short, overweight businessman with great wealth and influence in news-related media companies. He didn't speak much. His furry eyebrows had more of a personality than he did.

I hadn't realized that the Blackwood Forest was such a complex maze of mountainous trees, dense shrubbery, and winding trails. Sunlight shone down through the canopy above, casting shadows on the floor. The air was thick with the earthy fragrance of moss, damp soil, and pine. The humidity had everyone sweating. Omar Pierce was assigned to my search zone. I didn't mind his company. He was a good man with good morals. What you saw was what you got with him.

He was a police officer, and a close confidant of mine. He was tall, slender, and physically fit with bulging, veiny arms that stretched out his sleeves. He had a clean haircut and a freshly trimmed black beard. He was the same age as me, 35 years old. I was attracted to him, but my duty was to my children and to be a mother first. Besides, he had been good friends with my ex-husband. It complicated things.

"Do you think we're gonna find him?" Omar asked.

"We have to. He's just a kid. Even if he's a bully sometimes."

"He's still putting his hands on other students?"

"He put his hands on Layla," I said.

"That's Ethan's girlfriend. What the hell? Aren't they best friends? I'd never do something like that."

"I know. It's complicated, I guess. When I tell Ethan he'll just have to talk to Henry and work it out. He needs to set boundaries and Layla needs to tell Ethan what's been going on," I said.

"You'll step in if it's not resolved?" Omar asked.

"I will," I asserted.

Omar had always been a warm and welcome presence since the first time I met him. That was ages ago. When I was still married to Felix. It was obvious that Omar liked me, but he never did anything. He was respectful of my relationship with Felix. They stopped being friends after he found out what happened. He was as shocked as I was and hated Felix just as much as I did.

"It doesn't surprise me that Henry is that way. The apple doesn't fall far from the tree. Just look at Lawrence and Veronica. Two despicable people who you can't stand and who you wish would just go away forever," Omar said.

"You're not wrong."

"I still can't believe Lawrence forgave her for cheating," Omar said.

"I can. He probably has a dozen mistresses. Who knows what goes on in that marriage if you can even call it that."

"He can almost be her daddy. I'm disgusted. I'm gonna puke," Omar fake puked on me as we laughed.

"He could've been her dad when they met. She was like 18 and he was 40."

"My god, imagine having a kid with a 40-year-old at 18. I'm really gonna vomit, Sonya."

"Veronica has always been after the money. It doesn't surprise me that she locked that man down," I scoffed.

Veronica and I used to be best friends a long time ago. We even got pregnant with our firstborns around the same time. We bonded over that.

"How are the kids?"

"Santi's great and Ethan's good but he's been acting more rebellious than usual. I'm worried because of the situation with Henry."

"He's a good kid. I've seen it. He'll be okay."

"I also have to account for the divorce and how hard it's been on them," I sighed.

"Do they know the reason yet for the divorce?"

"I think they've figured it out. I tried to hide it, but you can't really hide things like that from your kids. Santi is so observant. Nothing gets past him."

"At least they know which parent to blame."

I was married to Felix for 10 years before he committed the ultimate betrayal. Willow had seen them. When she told me what they had done, I had an emotional meltdown. I was a complete mess. The relationship hadn't been going well, but I had the desire to fix things. After that, that desire went out the window. The marriage was terminated. He cheated on me with my best friend. There was no coming back from that. I was done with them both, forever.

"*We found something; you need to get over here quick. We're six hundred feet east of the green marker, over.*" An officer informed Omar over his walkie-talkie.

"*On my way, over and out,*" Omar responded.

"What's happening?" I asked.

"I can't be sure yet."

We rushed over to the location the officer indicated, and saw a massive swarm of the search party trying to get a look over a hillside where a ravine flowed. A dozen officers were escorting the search party volunteers away from the hillside and a few other cops were setting up a perimeter with yellow tape. My stomach formed a gut-wrenching knot. Something horrific had happened, the air was thick with grief. That much was very clear. Omar's stony face said it all.

"Oh no," he gasped.

An ear-shattering shrieking sliced through the air, and echoed throughout the Blackwood. It was the most tragic sound I had ever heard. Omar and I rushed forward to see what it was. It was Veronica. She was on the ground, pounding on the floor. Her face was beet-red, and she was wailing uncontrollably.

Lawrence sat beside her, and his face was deathly grim. A few tears rolled down his cheeks as he tried to console his wife. Felix was standing behind him, head hanging. He looked absolutely defeated. Omar slowly walked over to him as I followed closely behind.

"Felix?" Omar whispered.

"We found him," Felix whispered as he made a cutthroat gesture.

Omar grimly nodded and took me out of the yellow-tape zone.

"He's dead. He's dead, Sonya," Omar grimaced.

"Jesus Christ," I choked out, my hand over my mouth.

"It looks like it could be murder."

"Murder? Henry was *murdered*?" I asked.

"This isn't going to end well," Omar said gravely.

"Oh my god. This is horrible. Henry is dead. What? That's insane. He's just a teenager."

I didn't even know what to think. Henry Cain was dead, presumed murdered. But who would murder him? And why? Veronica's guttural screaming was so loud it seemed to ruffle the branches on the trees. A mother grieving for her dead child. There was nothing worse in this world. I thought about Ethan and Santi. No. It would never happen, ever. I wouldn't even dare to think of the possibility. I crossed it from my mind immediately.

"I gotta go help deal with all this. I'll see you later. You should head home before things get uglier."

He gave me a quick side hug and ran off to join the other officers. I was left mortified.

Henry Cain was dead. Veronica's son. Lawrence's son. Ethan's best friend. My student. A star athlete. Murdered?

Across the darkened grassy field, amidst the chaos of everything, I spotted a familiar face. It was Layla. I hadn't noticed her before. I didn't even know she was going to the search party. Ethan wasn't there so I found that to be pretty bizarre. She looked at me and had the most guilt-ridden expression I had ever seen from her. She looked like she had just committed a horrible crime. I was about to give her a wave before she snatched her eyes off mine and disappeared into the moving crowd.

Why was Layla there? Did she know something?

CHAPTER 5

I was in my car speeding to Felix's house. I didn't care if he still had his time with them. I didn't care if there was a huge fight anymore. I needed to speak with Ethan. Henry Cain was dead for Christ's sake. Ethan had to know something.

I had called Felix beforehand, so he was already outside, prepared to shoo me away. He was a fairly tall, potbellied man with mocha-colored skin and wavy dark hair. He usually sported a goatee and a set of designer sunglasses. I parked in his driveway, blocking his police cruiser. I already saw him groaning and moaning. I swung my door open and stormed to the front entrance. Felix cut off my path.

"Hey, hey, hey. What do you think you're doing, Sonya?" Felix asked.

"I need to speak with my son."

"Move your damn car, Sonya. I gotta go to work in an hour," Felix said, the irritation palpable in his voice.

"I won't be long," I stated.

"You know you really can't be here."

"I don't care. These are special circumstances. Henry Cain has been murdered."

"How the hell do you know that? That's not public information," Felix blurted out.

"You just told me."

"Oh my god. Omar told you, didn't he? That idiot. I'm gonna get him suspended."

"It was obvious, Felix. You could hear Veronica's wailing from 10 miles away."

"Why the hell are you even here?"

"I need to speak with Ethan. How many times do I need to tell you?"

"Yes, I know! But *why*? Why do you need to speak with him?!"

"Ethan's best friend was Henry. He's obviously going to be very shocked and confused. He needs me. He needs his mother."

"Go do what you need to do. Just please hurry, Sonya. I need to go. It's a shit show down at the station," Felix pleaded.

"Thank you," I said as I brushed past him.

"Also, you're not as tough as you think you are, okay? I'd slow your roll if I were you. You're not a hero," Felix chuckled.

"I am tough. I managed to tolerate you for 10 years without blowing my brains out," I snapped.

"Oh, that's real classy!" he yelled out.

I saw Santi in the living room playing on his iPad and ruffled his hair.

"Sorry you had to hear that, sweetheart."

"It's okay. Dad is such a jerk sometimes. He doesn't know how to be nice to people," Santi muttered.

My 13-year-old-son had better sense than a grown ass man. It was pathetic.

"Where's your brother?"

"He's in his room. Is everything okay?" Santi asked shakily.

"Honestly, no. Everything is not okay right now," I replied.

"Oh. Why?" Santi asked.

"You'll know soon. Don't worry, it'll turn out fine. Just trust your mom."

"I do trust you, mom."

I knocked on Ethan's door.

"It's your mom. Open up, Ethan."

He swung it open and welcomed me inside.

"Thank you for allowing me in for once."

"Yeah, it's cool," Ethan shrugged.

"What were you doing?"

"I was thinking about my doomed existence on this planet."

"Why? Are you alright?"

"I was kidding, mom."

"Please don't scare me like that."

"I'm sorry."

Ethan's room was interesting. The walls had posters featuring alternative bands, rebellious slogans, and *alternative* artwork. Graffiti-style murals of famous basketball players, indie band stickers, and a hand-made collage of magazine clippings covered portions of the wall above his bed frame. The lighting in the room was dim and moody, with lava lamps and colored bulbs giving off a warm glow. The shelves were loaded with graphic novels, artistic trinkets and a steel book of action shots featuring him in his high school games. He was a rebel alright. A rebel and proud. He had the exact same setup at my house. I awkwardly sat down on a bean bag while he smirked, and sat on his bed.

"Are you laughing at me?"

"No," Ethan giggled.

"How are you feeling?"

"I'm okay."

"I need to talk to you about something serious."

"Oh god," Ethan grumbled.

"Ethan, have you heard about Henry?"

He stayed quiet and sighed.

"Yeah I've heard the rumors. Is he really dead?"

"Yes. Henry is dead."

"Holy shit. That's crazy. It doesn't even feel real," Ethan remarked, rubbing his watery eyes.

"I know."

"How the hell did he die?"

"The police believe he was murdered."

"Murdered? Who would kill him? That's insane."

"I don't know, but I am worried."

"Why?"

"Your teammate Jonathan Locke was arrested recently by the police. When they were dragging him away, he shouted out that you and Henry hated each other. Can you explain why he would say something like that?"

"It's not important."

"Ethan, please tell me."

"Okay look, we weren't as close as you thought. Obviously I'm really sad and shocked that he's dead but we weren't that close towards the end. Our friendship fizzled out."

"Why? What happened? Does this have something to do with Layla?"

Ethan sat up and gave me a curious look.

"What do you know about him and Layla?"

"Well, he put his hands on her and was teasing her. It was very inappropriate. It was strange because I thought he was your best friend. Best friends don't do that to each other."

Ethan nodded and punched his bed. I jumped. He usually didn't do things like that. He wasn't prone to violent outbursts. At least I thought he wasn't.

"Alright mom, Henry was kind of a bully. He was cool sometimes, but other times he would act like a real prick. So, I don't know. It was up and down. I mean, I was forced to be friends with him because of basketball. We were always on the same team, so it always came back to that. We're brothers for life through basketball. That's what he would say."

"I get it, son."

"It got worse when I started dating Layla. I guess he secretly liked her or something, but he started messing with her way too much. I got pissed, you know?"

"You already knew he was touching her."

"Yeah, I knew."

"What ended up happening?"

"I fought with him. We fought, physically. It wasn't that bad. It was a stupid scuffle," Ethan shrugged.

"Jesus, Ethan. When was this?"

"It was pretty recent. Maybe a day or two before his death."

"Oh my god, Ethan. Do you know how this is gonna look? This looks really bad."

If the police question me, I'm not telling them anything. I know nothing of a fight, and they were best friends. End of story. I don't know who to trust and from now on, all that matters is making sure my son remains innocent.

"I know, mom. I know. I'm pretty freaking scared to be honest."

"I figured. Santi told me you were nervous about something, and you also missed school. Did you know this was gonna happen?"

"No, I didn't know anything. I swear."

"So Jonathan Locke was right."

"He's an idiot, but yeah. He was right."

"He's gonna tell the police that you two fought."

"He worshipped Henry. He's definitely telling them."

"Ethan, nothing leaves this room."

"I didn't kill him, mom. How can you even think that? I'm your son."

"I haven't asked that."

"It's obvious you were going there."

"I wasn't going to ask that but thank you for your answer."

"What would you even do, if I did do it?"

"I would do everything in my power to save you."

"Wait, really? You wouldn't turn me in?"

"Absolutely not. You're my son. You're not going anywhere."

Ethan stood up and leaped over to give me a hug.

"This shit is so scary, mom. I can't believe he's dead. He's just gone." Ethan started sobbing.

"It's very tragic, Ethan."

"He was so young, you know? I literally talked with him that day at practice. We were goofing off with the other guys. Now he's dead? What the hell is going on?" Ethan asked.

He was crying so hard; he drenched my shoulder with his tears.

"This is so bad, mom. Who would murder him like that? I'm losing my shit," Ethan whispered.

"I know, baby. It's okay. I got you. We'll get through this together. I promise you."

Innocent or guilty.

All the local news outlets were reporting it and it was official. The Skyview PD were treating Henry's death as a homicide. It was absolutely shocking to say the least. The entire town felt like it was in mourning. Many high school basketball media sites were posting tributes and highlight tapes of Henry's best plays when he played at Skyview.

Everyone was given directions to attend the gym after attendance was called. The school was holding a memorial for Henry. We passed Mr. Griffin's class on the way over there and when I glanced inside, I saw that he was oddly rummaging through all the filing cabinets in his classroom. He was practically turning the whole room upside down, looking for something. I instructed my class to behave and to go on without me. Thankfully they listened. Mostly because their classmate was dead. At least they had some sense of respect. I peeked inside Mr. Griffin's room and slightly opened the door. When he saw me, he sprang up from the floor and gave me a big smile.

"Hello Ms. Salvador! What can I do for you?" Mr. Griffin asked.

"I just wanted to let you know that the memorial for Henry is starting soon in the gym. They told you right?" I asked.

"Oh, yes! I'm on my way. They didn't forget the old goat this time," Mr. Griffin laughed.

"Oh, alright. I'll see you there. I know how fond you were of Henry."

"Oh my god, yes. It's so tragic. I loved him very much. He was a good kid. He had a strong body for his age. Hell of a player."

I nodded and continued on my way. Some say Mr. Griffin was a bit *too* fond of Henry. That had been said not one or two times either. It was said multiple times. When I got to the gym, it felt like a ghost town. Row after row was filled to the brim with students but not a peep was heard. They had Henry's jersey hanging from the rafters and his picture was up on a massive projector screen. Willow, Veronica, Lawrence, Coach Albert, the basketball team, and the school's administration stood side by side near the podium, ready to pay their respects. Felix, Omar and two other police officers were standing guard. Felix and Omar kept a healthy distance from each other.

I sat near the other English teachers who were silently gossiping about who could've killed Henry. I rolled my eyes and tuned them out. I saw Ethan walking in with Layla as they held hands. He was very sweet with her, and I knew for a fact that he would never lay his hands on her. He was not that type of boy. Henry, on the other hand, who knew?

Ethan kissed Layla then went to join the rest of his team who patted him on the back. It seemed like they were all intent on leaning on each other after what happened. Jonathan Locke was noticeably absent and was most likely still in police custody.

Veronica rose up to the podium and looked understandably grief-stricken. She had dark circles around her eyes and constantly sniffled. She cleared her throat and adjusted the mic. They played Henry's basketball highlights on the projector as she talked.

"I loved Henry, my only son, more than anything else in this world. From the moment he was born he gave us so much joy. He was a happy baby who laughed at everything. My heart warmed whenever I saw my baby boy. I just…I can't believe he's gone. Every day I wake up, thinking it's a nightmare but it's real…and it's never-ending. I'll never be the same again. I was supposed to watch him grow up, go to college, get married, have children, and follow his dreams of being a professional basketball player. It was all ripped from him so cruelly. He was loved by so many. He was loved by his teachers, his classmates, his teammates and his best friend, Ethan Salvador. We love you, Ethan. We know you share this pain and this grief with us. We know you miss him so much. We know you loved him like a brother," Veronica expressed while she gloomily looked at Ethan.

He nodded and put a fist to his heart. Veronica did the same.

"He always told me you guys were brothers for life." Veronica began to cry. She couldn't hold it in anymore and doubled over. She collapsed to the ground and sobbed. Lawrence hoisted her up and softly escorted her away from the podium.

"I'm very sorry, everyone. Please forgive my wife. We are going through something unimaginable. The pain has been unrelenting, and we are trying our best to live for Henry," Lawrence icily stated.

It sure doesn't look like it.

Has he even cried?

That man is a block of stone.

The English teachers whispered things that reminded me why I wasn't friends with them. All people grieve in their own ways. After

Veronica spoke, Willow went, and then the rest of the school's administration followed. They ended the ceremony by having the team repeat sayings that Henry would shout out at the beginning of school games.

One team. One goal.
We grind together, we shine together.
I want cheesy nachos.
Remember guys, winning isn't everything, it's the only thing!
Win or lose, I love this team. Skyview Suns forever.

Ethan went up last and capped it off.

Brothers for life.

Ethan's eyes grew watery as he left the podium. It was rare for him to cry. Despite everything that had happened, I believed Ethan did love Henry like a brother at one point in time. There was no way in hell he would *murder* him. That was an act done out of pure hatred, and anger. Ethan didn't have a heart made of ice. As the ceremony ended, the entire student body shuffled out of the gym. The sun blinded me for a second as I stepped outside. When I regained vision, Omar was standing outside with two other cops. They looked apprehensive. A hand then grabbed my arm and pulled me aside. I quickly glanced to my right and saw Felix.

"Felix? What the hell are you doing? Let go of me," I demanded as I tried to push him off.

"Sonya, I'm gonna need you to relax for a second. Okay?" Felix asked.

"What? What's going on?"

As soon as Ethan stepped out, Omar approached him with handcuffs.

"I'm sorry son, but you're being placed under arrest."

"Hey! What the hell is going?!" I shouted.

I lunged forward, but Felix pulled me back and bear hugged me. The more I struggled, the more he restrained me.

"Felix, that is our son! Do something! Why is he being arrested?!" I shrieked.

"I'm sorry, Sonya. I can't mess with this. It's police business."

He couldn't even look me in the eye.

"Mom? Dad? What's going on?" Ethan asked as he tried to stay away from Omar.

"It's okay, baby. It's gonna be okay. Omar, seriously?! What is this?!"

"I'm sorry. I'll explain later, Sonya. He's gonna be okay, I promise you."

"No, get away from me. You're not arresting me."

"Son, I know you and you know me. I'm gonna help you out. Please bear with me. I know this is scary," Omar urged as he reached out with the handcuffs. Ethan swatted his hands away and punched him in the face. Omar flinched backwards and held his jaw.

"Jesus, kid. I'm trying to help you!"

"You're trying to arrest me! How is that helping me, Omar?!"

"Ethan don't hit them! Stop it! You don't hit them!" I commanded.

"Mom, why are they arresting me?!"

"I don't know, sweetie. I don't know."

"Felix, tell your son what's going on! What kind of father are you?!"

He remained quiet. I couldn't believe what was happening. My son was being arrested while hundreds of students were watching. Willow was horrified, and was ordered back when she tried to interject. The entire basketball team yelled at the cops to let my son go, but it was no use. The two cops with Omar tackled Ethan to the ground and forced the handcuffs on him. Omar pushed them off Ethan before they hurt him.

"Hey! I said I was taking point on this. Don't hurt him, he's just a kid!" Omar shouted as he lifted Ethan off the ground.

"Please let him be okay. Please," I pleaded.

"You need to trust me, Sonya. It's gonna be okay."

"Mom, am I going to jail?"

"It's not like that, son. You shouldn't have resisted arrest. We just need to ask some questions," Omar promised.

"I love you, Ethan. I'm gonna get you out. I promise. Stay safe and don't fight them unless you absolutely have to."

"Mom get them away from me! This is bullshit! I didn't do anything wrong!" Ethan shouted.

They took him through the uproarious crowd, to the parking lot and into a police cruiser. Willow and the school administration yelled at everyone to get to class. Meanwhile, I was hysterical. I ripped myself out of Felix's grasp, turned and slapped him in the face so hard it left a bright red mark on his cheek. He cried out in pain, and staggered backwards. He glared at me with rage-filled eyes. I glared at him back and dared him to do something. He broke off eye contact and rubbed his cheek.

"I could arrest you too, Sonya. You would go away for a long time," Felix threatened.

"I'm not afraid of you, Felix. That's not the first time you've said that. When are you gonna deliver on your promise?" I asked.

"Don't test me, Sonya. You won't like how it ends," Felix warned.

"Why did the police arrest our son and why didn't you do anything about it?"

"He's a suspect."

"What?"

"They think Ethan murdered Henry Cain."

CHAPTER 6

The inside of the police station was a busy environment filled with multiple cops, and government personnel. It had an open floor plan with various computer workstations and telecommunications systems used by IT workers, detectives, traffic cops, dispatchers and more.

Offices and interview rooms were located throughout the station, providing spaces for officers to conduct private conversations, and interviews. Holding cells securely held individuals who had been arrested or detained. That's where Ethan was, sitting next to actual criminals and violent offenders. I sat in the reception area waiting for the police to inform me about my son. Felix paced back and forth.

"Can't you find out what's going on?"

"Not really, Sonya. It's a conflict of interest. Please use your head for once."

"You're insufferable," I scoffed.

Felix rolled his eyes and turned his back to me. I was having the worst day of my life inside that police station. My bubbling anxiety was palpable in my stomach, forming knots that grew tighter with each passing minute. I felt like I couldn't breathe.

"Ethan couldn't have possibly killed Henry. He's a good kid. He gets in trouble sometimes, but he's not a killer."

"We'll see."

"What the hell are you saying? This is our son. We know him. He would *never* do something like this."

"I know that Sonya. Just let the police do what they need to do."

"Why do you act like you don't even know him? He's not a stranger."

"Can you please be quiet? I can't even hear myself think," Felix whined.

"Thank you for that."

"You're welcome."

"Why aren't we allowed in the room if they're questioning him?"

"They're allowed to question him alone. Okay? It's protocol."

"Since when?"

"Since, I don't know, a long time. I wasn't there when they came up with the damn policy."

Absolutely useless.

An officer came out to address us.

"Hey Stanley, my buddy, what's going on in there? What can you tell us?"

"We're gonna be holding him for a while longer. We'll let you know when you can see him," Officer Stanley said.

"Why are you holding him longer? On what grounds?"

"Ma'am, I'm very sorry but as you can imagine this is a very time-sensitive case and we cannot disclose any more details at this time. Henry's justice is at stake," Officer Stanley said.

"Oh, c'mon man. That's my son in there. I'm a cop. We can't make something happen?"

"You know how much deep shit we would be in? We'd lose our jobs," Officer Stanley scoffed.

"I know, I know. I had to try," Felix offered as he shrugged at me.

"Thanks Felix. What a *valiant* effort."

"I don't need this from you. I tried. Nothing is ever enough for you."

"Be quiet. Officer Stanley, can you please inform me when my son will be released? I can't be here forever. I have to pick up my other son from school."

"I'm sorry, but I cannot. It's a very sensitive case," Officer Stanley declared.

"Yes, you've mentioned that it's very sensitive. Where is Officer Omar Pierce? I need to speak with him," I demanded.

"He's busy right now," Officer Stanley answered.

"Is he the one questioning my son?" I asked.

"You know I can't answer that."

"Why are you asking about your little boyfriend?"

"Oh, that's rich coming from you."

"I need to head back. We'll have more information soon, thank you," Officer Stanley said as he marched away.

"Shove your information up your—," I trailed.

"I'm sorry, what was that?" Felix asked.

"Forget this, I'm calling a lawyer," I said as I took out my phone.

"I told you; it's no use if he isn't being charged with anything."

"You're only saying that because you don't wanna pay for it."

"That's not true."

"They're questioning him. Our son needs legal counsel. It's not up for debate."

"I highly doubt they're questioning him now. They're still getting their facts straight."

"It's fine. I'll pay for it. How much gambling debt are you in?"

"Shut up, Sonya. You know I have issues. I was diagnosed," Felix said.

"Trust me, I know you have issues."

"I've taught Ethan what to do in these situations. A lawyer is not necessary."

"I'm not listening to you."

"You never do. Why do I even try?" Felix said throwing his hands up in the air.

I ended up calling Arthur Faraday, a family friend, who arrived within the hour. He was a slim, older gentleman with a luscious set of gelled grey hair. He wore a professional suit, with brown dress shoes and silver horn-rimmed glasses. I knew I could call him because he always meant business. He greeted us and Felix reluctantly greeted him back.

"How much do you charge per hour, sir?" Felix asked.

"Don't answer him, I'm the one paying you."

"I need to be informed."

"You don't need to be informed of anything. Stop acting like a child, Felix."

"You see how she is with me?"

"We can sort out all the payment details later. For now, I want to go in, find your son and figure out what the hell is going on," Arthur said as he strode right into the police station. An officer blocked his path and asked him to state his business.

"My name is Arthur Faraday. I am an attorney representing the interests of Ethan Salvador. You have him in your custody and have not allowed either parent to accompany their child who is a minor. I assume he's not being questioned yet because that is extremely illegal and whatever case you may be building will be promptly thrown out the window by me. So you will let me in before I raise hell in this department," Arthur commanded.

The officer stepped aside and allowed Arthur entry. He turned around and gave a thumbs up.

"This won't take long, Sonya. We'll be in and out," Arthur said.

"Thank you, Arthur!"

I wish Felix would take command like that.

I waited two more hours. Felix had already left to go to work. I had to pick up Santi and take him to the police station with me. He asked me a million questions about Ethan.

Why did they arrest him?

Where is he?

Do they really think he killed him?

Is Ethan going to jail?

Truthfully, I didn't have a lot of answers to his questions which frightened me. I had to stay strong and put on a brave face for him. When we got back to the station, Arthur was waiting for me outside. I didn't see Ethan with him so that immediately filled me with worry. I parked, told Santi to stay put, got out of the car, and rushed to Arthur.

"Tell me, Arthur. What happened?" I asked.

"First off, Ethan is okay and he's in good spirits since he obviously knows he didn't murder Henry Cain. He says he loves you and wants to come home," Arthur explained.

"Oh, Arthur. Why isn't my son out here? What's going on?" I asked.

"I'm so sorry, Sonya but they've applied to hold him for 72 hours. They sincerely believe your son murdered Henry," Arthur admitted.

"Oh god. Why? What do they even have?" I asked.

"They believe they have probable cause because his alibi is a bit shaky. He said he was with his girlfriend, Layla, after practice and then he went home that night when Henry was murdered. They think it's possible that he could've gone to the Blackwood Forest in between Layla's house and your house. They're establishing a timeline and they're testing dried specks of blood that was found on his hands. My guess is, they think it belongs to Henry," Arthur said.

"That's ridiculous. He wouldn't go from Layla's house to the Blackwood. He came straight home. When will we know if it's Henry's blood?"

"In approximately two days."

"So, they're pretty much holding him until those results come back."

"Precisely. There's something else," Arthur said as he pulled out his phone.

He played a video of Ethan fighting Henry on the basketball court. It got very ugly with punches and kicks being thrown. They looked like they wanted to maul each other.

"Ethan told me it was a stupid scuffle. I'm gonna kill him."

"Is there something I should know, Sonya? Is something else gonna be revealed? I don't like surprises. This is very alarming," Arthur said.

I genuinely didn't know and that terrified me.

"Ethan doesn't have any more secrets, Arthur."

"Well, okay. We'll just have to wait and see how it all plays out."

"Any reason you didn't bring me into the room when they were questioning him?" I asked.

"I find that it's best to let me handle that. This was just a preliminary questioning session. Sonya, they don't have any other suspects so naturally they're going after Ethan and they're trying to come up with a case that more than likely doesn't exist. Yes there's evidence they went at each other's throats, but we could easily argue that was basketball-related and in the heat of the moment. Now, I have to ask again, are you sure there's nothing else I should know?" Arthur asked.

"I'm sure," I lied.

I can't tell you something I don't know, and do I think Ethan has more secrets? Unfortunately, yes.

"Okay, well listen Sonya, I think your son is gonna be fine. From what I can tell they don't have a murder weapon either. They're scrambling. Henry Cain was a very popular star athlete, and this case is highly publicized. They're trying to make themselves look good," Arthur said.

"I hope he gets out of there okay. This type of stuff traumatizes a kid. Imagine being arrested and accused of the murder of your best friend when you're only 16-years-old."

"He'll need you every step of the way," Arthur added.

I grimly nodded. I knew it was gonna be a tough task, but I was ready. I had to be. Omar came out and pointed at me.

"Hey, Sonya. Sorry about all this. It's a part of my job unfortunately. Can we talk? Just you and me?"

I looked to Arthur who gave a thumbs up.

"You know what to say and what not to say, I presume?"

"I do. He's a longtime friend. It'll be fine."

I had love and respect for Omar as a friend, but I wasn't planning on telling him a god damn thing. I couldn't take the chance. Ethan came first. My children always came first.

I sat in a hard metal chair in a grey, square box of a room that felt like a prison. The central light perched to the ceiling gave off a low humming, white glow that screamed isolation. I was positioned across Omar.

Omar was a man who told me many things I shouldn't have known. He had a soft spot for me. He knew I'd never rat him out. As a result, I became privy to important information that aided me in the aftermath of the terrible crime that my son had been accused of.

"Are you sure we should be considering this?" I asked.

"We have to, Sonya. Like it or not, your son is a suspect," Omar sighed.

"I told you already, he was with me that night at home. He came right after his practice ended. He had no reason to go through the Blackwood."

"They still think it's a bit shaky given the other evidence. They believe he could've done it before he went home. He had time."

I folded my arms as I tried to suppress my rising frustration.

"This is insane, Omar. He wouldn't do this."

"They believe Ethan has specks of Henry's blood on his hands."

I almost fell off the chair as I lunged forward.

"What? That's not possible. Why would he have his blood on his hands?" I asked.

"They had gotten into a fight at school, shortly before Henry's murder. That's why he was arrested, Sonya. Ethan's fingerprints are on Henry's body. Your lawyer knows all this."

"No, no, no. Ethan has never gotten into a fight. Who the hell told you that?" I asked.

"Multiple eyewitnesses saw it happen during a basketball practice."

"Oh please, Omar. It's basketball. They get physical all the time with each other. *It's how the game is played*. Those are Ethan's words."

"It wasn't just an altercation. They swung at each other."

"What the hell? Why am I hearing about this now?"

"I think the coach wanted to keep it under wraps. He didn't want Ethan or Henry getting suspended."

"Jesus Christ. I'm gonna kill Ethan."

"Look, they had probable cause to arrest him, but they need more. Your lawyer can argue that since they play basketball six days out of the week, it's not out of the ordinary for Ethan to have his DNA on Henry. The blood thing can be tossed out too."

"Are you sure?"

"It's insufficient evidence. What they really need to do is recover the murder weapon and get the prints off of that."

"What do they think is the murder weapon?" I asked.

"A switchblade or a box cutter. Some kind of handy knife with a razor-sharp blade," Omar answered.

"How did he die exactly?"

"He was stabbed in the throat multiple times and then thrown onto a big rock from up above. Henry's spine was in half. It's gruesome, Sonya. The poor kid had a future. He could really play basketball like your son."

"I feel sorry for Veronica."

"It's a terrible loss."

"Did you guys ever find Henry's phone?" I asked.

"We did and it was completely destroyed. It's no use."

"That's a big blow. A teenager hides many secrets in their phone."

"Do you think Ethan has secrets in his phone?"

"Are you guys gonna search through it?" I asked.

"We need a warrant first."

"You guys are ruthless. He's just a kid."

"Sonya, can you think of any reason why Ethan would murder Henry? Did he ever tell you bad things about him? Did he ever get into arguments with him?" Omar asked.

"As far as I know, they were best friends. So, I don't understand this fight they got into. It must've been a short scuffle between friends. Anything else doesn't make sense to me."

It was true. Ethan and Henry Cain had been best friends since childhood. They grew up playing basketball together. They were on the same teams and went through the same highs and lows. They won a state championship in middle school and lost 9 pick-up games in a row at the local park. They had been through it all.

"Well, if they can't pinpoint a motive it'll be harder to prosecute."

"He shouldn't even be in this situation to begin with. He's only sixteen. He's a good boy. A great boy, Omar. Yeah, he gets in trouble sometimes and he can be rebellious, but he's got a good heart. All he does is go to school, play basketball, and go out with his girlfriend. He does not stab people in the neck or throw them onto big rocks. That's crazy. He's not a murderer."

"You don't need to convince me. You need to convince everyone else," Omar said gravely.

I sighed and pinched my nose. I stared down at the floor.

How did it all go so wrong?

CHAPTER 7

While I anxiously waited for Ethan to be released, I had to go back to work and attempt to be normal. *Normal.* I scoffed at the idea. Nothing was normal for me at that time. I was having the worst period of my entire life. It was worse than my divorce from Felix, and worse than finding out he had been cheating on me with Veronica Cain. When I walked through the hallway at the school, I saw a large crowd forming near Ethan's locker which had been cordoned off with yellow tape.

What now?

Omar was there with a couple of other officers shooing away students. I approached him.

"Hey, what are you doing here?"

"Hey Sonya. You shouldn't be here. There's evidence we need to collect."

"Evidence of what? Why are you even searching through his locker?"

"We got an anonymous tip."

"Of what?"

"We'll talk later."

I was forced to walk away as they investigated my son's locker. God knows what was in there. Ethan was making things hard for me, but I had to uphold my faith in him. As I passed the cafeteria, I spotted Santi crying in a corner outside. I rushed over to him and grabbed his arm.

"Hey, sweetheart. What's wrong?" I asked.

"They're saying Ethan's a killer. They're saying Ethan murdered Henry." Santi choked out.

"Oh baby, no. They're wrong. Who's telling you that?" I asked.

"They're mostly older kids who walk by and tell me that my brother is a murderer and that he should die," Santi said.

"Jesus, kids can be cruel. Do you know who they were?" I asked.

"Mom, I have no idea. I'm sorry. I'm so sorry. I should've said something, but there was so many of them. They were scaring me," Santi sobbed.

I gave him a tight hug and massaged his hair.

"Mom, people are gonna see."

"I don't care, I'm your mother."

"It's *cringey*," Santi groaned.

"You're crying by yourself in a corner. That's *cringey*."

I managed to get a hearty laugh out of him.

"You're not wrong."

"Listen to me, I don't want you to pay attention to what anyone says about Ethan, okay? You know him and I know him. We are his family. He is my son; he is your brother. Do you think he's a murderer?"

"No, of course not."

"Exactly, so ignore them and tell them to go to hell."

"Okay, mom. I will."

"Now get to class before I tell people you wet the bed until you were 8 years old."

Santi giggled and ran off. I couldn't believe they were bullying Santi because of what Ethan *allegedly* did. Kids were the worst sometimes. I got a text from Omar asking me to meet him in the courtyard during lunch. We met in a secluded area underneath the shade of a tree and sat on a stone bench.

"Good hiding spot."

"Thanks," Omar said.

"What did you guys find in my son's locker?"

"I'll be honest with you, Sonya. It's not looking good. We found a box cutter caked with blood. We're getting it tested at the lab."

I began to rapidly breathe in and out. I was on the verge of another panic attack.

Why is this happening to him? Why?!

Omar rubbed my back to comfort me.

"Sonya, calm down. We don't know who's blood is on the box cutter."

"Would it even matter? Why does my son have a box cutter with blood in his locker?"

"That's what I want to know."

"Someone must've planted it there. There's no way Ethan would have that."

"Or maybe he was hiding it for someone."

"What are you thinking?"

"I don't know. I don't think Ethan killed Henry, but maybe he knows who did, and he's trying to protect them."

"Well, I don't know what to tell you. I don't think he would get himself involved with that stuff. He's not that type of kid."

"We'll just have to wait for the DNA results."

"Omar, you have to help me prove his innocence. You know he didn't do this."

"The evidence is stacking up against him, Sonya. I don't know. The lead detective on this is adamant that he murdered him. Now, that we have a potential murder weapon in his locker, it'd make a compelling case in the court room."

"I'm telling you there has to be another reason he had that in there."

"We're checking the security cameras to make sure nobody was messing with his locker. We'll find out the truth, Sonya."

"What can I do to help on this?"

"I don't know. Do you have any other information you can share?"

"Not really, no."

"The only way to get the heat off Ethan is to find another suspect who was more likely to murder Henry that night."

"What about Jonathan Locke? You guys arrested him before Ethan. What's going on with him?"

"I'm not completely sure, but it seems that Ethan is more likely to be the culprit than Jonathan at the moment. They might be releasing him soon. The lead detective is tight-lipped on him. I have to see how it plays out."

"What happens if I find another suspect then?"

"I'm not sure if I'd be willing to look into it. My boss has all resources focused on Ethan."

"I'll do it myself then."

"I don't think that's a good idea, Sonya."

"I'm not gonna stand around and wait until my son is falsely charged with Henry's murder. Ethan's entire life hangs in the balance. I will prove his innocence, with or without you," I said as I stormed off.

"Sonya, come on. I'll try to help you. You don't have to act so tough all the time."

I ignored him as I wracked my brain, thinking of someone who could've possibly killed Henry that night. I went on autopilot mode while teaching my classes and couldn't wait for the school day to be over. I had Santi stay after school to play basketball with some friends while I put my plan into action. I didn't know if I would be successful or not, but I had to try. I waltzed into Mr. Griffin's classroom and was immediately put off by the dimmed lighting. He was silently grading papers at his desk until I knocked on his door. He glanced up.

"Oh, hey Sonya. What can I do for you?"

"Hey, Griffin, I just wanted to stop by and say hello."

"That's very kind of you. Hey, listen, I'm so sorry to hear all that stuff about your son. He's still being held in police custody?"

"He is."

"Good golly, miss molly. I hope he's released soon. It's ridiculous. Ethan would never kill Henry. It was such a gruesome murder too with a box cutter. If I think about it too much, I start shaking all over."

"A box cutter, huh? How do you know that was the murder weapon?"

"Oh, you know, they released it online or whatever. I heard the police came by and confiscated it from someone's locker. It could be speculation for all I know."

I should've questioned him further on that point, but I already had a plan in mind. I didn't want to stray away from it.

"I've always been curious, Mr. Griffin, how come you don't coach the baseball team anymore?"

"Well, I got too old for it and decided to retire."

"That's not what I heard."

"Oh, what did you hear then?" Mr. Griffin asked with a chuckle.

"I heard you like teenage boys."

"How do you mean? I'm not following."

"I meant in the *sexual* sense," I enunciated while glaring straight into his soul.

Mr. Griffin gaped at me and stammered for several seconds before answering.

"Absolutely not. I don't know what you're suggesting or what you're trying to get at, but it's crazy talk. Alright? That's crazy talk."

"Everyone knows how fond you were of Henry, Mr. Griffin."

"He was a good kid and one hell of an athlete. We used to talk about sports. What of it?"

I got closer to him and stared him down.

"I think you touched him."

"Excuse me? What the hell are you talking about?"

"I think you touched him in places he didn't want to be touched and when he threatened to expose you, you killed him."

Mr. Griffin was so shocked by the accusation that he could barely speak.

"Now I…I'd never, ever do that to somebody. Sonya, you are way out of line. I'm gonna speak to Principal Jacobson about this because this is very disrespectful. This is harassment!" Mr. Griffin exclaimed.

"You sexually abuse minors. You know I'm speaking the truth."

I'll admit it. It was an explosive accusation, and I didn't have any solid proof to back it up, but his reputation had lived on for a long time. Throughout the years many people have said he was touching minors. I didn't think everyone would be lying about that. I was so desperate to find Henry's murderer that I was willing to try anything to save my son. Even if it meant risking my career to get to the truth.

"Okay Sonya, I need you to leave right now. You are saying some very crazy things that are simply not true. I don't touch little boys. I am a happily married man. Are you insane?" Mr. Griffin asked as he got up.

"Then why has your secret reputation lived on for so long?"

"Kids like to talk a lot of smack. You should know that by now."

"What's that supposed to mean?"

"Whatever you think it's supposed to mean," Mr. Griffin snapped.

"Why were you rummaging through all your things the day of Henry's memorial? What were you looking for?"

"What? What are you talking about?"

"You know what I'm talking about. What were you looking for? Secret phone? Scandalous pictures? Confession letter?"

"Sonya, I need you to leave before things get ugly."

"Is that a threat?"

"*Go now*!" Mr. Griffin yelled.

"Just because you yell doesn't mean I'm afraid of you. You're not the first man who has tried that on me."

"That's great, Sonya. I know you think of yourself as some really tough, independent woman but I don't care. I don't care if you're feisty or aggressive by nature. I won't accept that as an excuse. You can keep it out of this classroom and away from me."

He had no idea what I was capable of. When he tried to tell me how I was as a person, it was over for him. I didn't take that lightly. He was finished.

"I'm not done with you, Mr. Griffin," I declared as I stormed out.

"Yes you are!" Mr. Griffin bellowed.

It didn't take long for Willow to catch up to me on the soccer field. I was walking through to the outdoor basketball courts to get Santi. Willow looked very annoyed.

"I can't believe you made me run in these heels."

"I'm sorry your highness, but I had to talk to Mr. Griffin."

"You didn't talk to him; you interrogated him and accused him of very serious sexual crimes."

"He's had that reputation for a very long time now. I just wanted to get the facts straight."

"It doesn't matter, Sonya. It's all rumors and gossip. No one has come out to accuse him of sexual assault."

"What if they were too afraid to? What if they didn't understand what was happening to them? He was a well-liked baseball coach. The power dynamic was in his favor. You can't expect growing teenagers to speak out when all they're taught is to obey the adults," I stressed.

"You can't go around accusing other teachers of being sexual predators without evidence, Sonya. That's a big problem."

"It's not a problem if it's true."

"You have no idea if it's true, Sonya. I could strangle you right now."

"Fine, you're right. I may have gone a little overboard, but I still have my suspicions."

"A little? You stormed a nice old man's classroom, and basically called him a child rapist to his face without backing it up."

"Okay, I see that now."

Willow grabbed my shoulder.

"It's fine. I know what you're going through. I kept the peace with him and reminded him about Ethan. He calmed down about it and it's water under the bridge. Please keep it that way," Willow urged.

"Okay. I will."

Willow had always been the diplomatic one. I was fire, she was water. She strived for peace, and I had no problem going to war if I needed to. I picked up Santi and we drove home. He was quiet during the entire ride.

"Everything okay, Santi?"

"Yeah," he mumbled as he gazed out the window.

He was still upset over Ethan. I knew the only thing that would make him feel better was his brother coming home. I felt the exact same way. The house felt emptier with him gone. He left behind a gaping black hole that was irreplaceable. When I parked at the house I noticed something strange on our front door.

"Santi, stay here for a second."

"Why? What's wrong? Is someone there?"

"Just give me a second," I said as I exited my car.

I slowly made my way over to the front door and took out my phone to use the flashlight. When I pointed it at the object, I jumped and almost fell backwards. Someone had used a large kitchen knife to pin a severed, bloody Halloween head on my front door. I angrily grabbed the knife and tossed it aside. I snatched the head before it fell to the floor and read what was inscribed on its forehead.

Ethan killed Henry. Ethan is a murderer. Maybe he got it from his mommy and daddy?

I hastily launched the bloody head across the front lawn before I remembered Santi was still in the car. I saw his shocked expression as he stared at the head, mortified. When I went to retrieve it, two black cars suddenly screeched in front of my house and put down their windows. I instinctually hid in front of my car as I heard what sounded like a volley of rocks being thrown all around my car and my house. A hundred sharp cracks and thuds reverberated all around me as I closed my eyes and waited for it to be over. I opened them and slowly peeked up to make sure Santi was safe through the windshield. He was trying to quickly untangle his seat belt, but I motioned for him to stay put. When it finally stopped, they decided to shout out a final message.

Ethan murdered Henry Cain! Accept the truth!

After they raced away, I saw blood dripping down my nose. Santi looked at me in shock and threw himself out of the car.

"Mom! Are you okay? What was that? Why were they throwing rocks at us?" Santi asked.

I touched my forehead and felt warm liquid spilling down. It felt like there was a small crater. I had gotten hit in the head during all the chaos. I grabbed a handkerchief out of my purse and pressed it to my fresh wound.

"I'm fine, sweetie. It's just a cut. I have no idea who those people were and why they threw rocks at us," I said.

I saw that there was at least a hundred rocks scattered all around my front yard. I locked my car and led Santi inside before anything else happened.

"What was that head? It looked like it was from Halloween."

"I don't know, son. People are trying to prank us, I guess."

The truth was it seemed like the town was turning against us. People were saying online that it was confirmed that Ethan had murdered

Henry, which I found to be absolutely ridiculous. He was being held in police custody, but he hadn't been charged yet. People didn't believe in innocent until proven guilty. They believed in sensationalist media narratives and gossip magazine propaganda. It was disgusting. They were talking about a young high school student with his entire life ahead of him. They wanted to destroy my beloved son's life before it even started. It was all for nothing. People didn't understand how much damage you could do spreading false rumors on the internet. It had the potential to scar people for life.

I told Santi he could play his video games so he could try and get his mind off of what happened. I went into the kitchen, poured myself a much-needed glass of wine and sat down on my couch. I tried to clear my head before calling Omar.

"*I was just about to call you.*"

"*What's up?*"

"*You go first.*"

"*You'll never believe what happened when I got home. Some teenagers left some severed Halloween head mask thing pinned to my front door with a kitchen knife.*"

"*Oh Christ, you've gotta be joking.*"

"*They inscribed something on it. They're saying Ethan is a murderer.*"

"*Those stupid kids are just trying to rattle you. Don't let them. They got nothing else better to do,*" Omar said.

"I wish I could just let it go, but two cars drove up to my house and started pelting rocks at me and my house. Santi was in the car, Omar. I got hit on my head. I even bled."

"Are you serious? Are you okay? Do you want me to come over? I'll take your statement. That's ridiculous. Those motherfuckers need to pay."

"I'm fine now, thank you Omar. I know I can always count on you," I said.

"Hey, you're a survivor, Sonya. You were forced to be one with all the shit you've been through and all the shit you're going through now."

"Yeah, I'm trying to stay strong."

"Listen, I have some news. We reviewed the security camera footage in the hallway where Ethan's locker is. We found something."

"What'd you find?" I asked.

"Ethan didn't put that box cutter in his locker."

I knew it.

"Who did it, Omar?"

"Jonathan Locke."

CHAPTER 8
BEFORE

There was a time when Felix and I were happily married. It was hard to believe, looking back. We regularly hung out with Veronica, Lawrence, and Henry at their beautiful summer home. It was a massive, Spanish-style house with large arched windows, a spacious open floor plan layered with cobblestone and a white stone exterior. It had a very sunny, intimate atmosphere as the entire house was draped in warm earth tones. It made you feel very welcome.

We usually did a backyard BBQ and sat near the lush vegetable garden that was adjacent to their glimmering swimming pool. Ethan, Santi, and Henry loved playing with the water hoop together. Those were the moments of pure, innocent bliss. The times before the cracks in our marriage began to show and widen. Felix usually aided Lawrence on his expensive grill since Lawrence didn't know how to use it very well. I sat on the wooden picnic bench with Veronica and drank freshly squeezed lemonade while we basked in the sun and took in the sizzling, charbroiled aroma of seasoned meats and chicken.

"This is what I live for Sonya. Who can stand being poor? No offense," Veronica giggled.

"You are not funny, bitch."

"No but seriously, being with Lawrence has been amazing. I know he was like 40 and I was 20 when we met but he's my soulmate. The age gap never mattered to us."

"You did have his child pretty quickly."

"You had Felix's pretty quickly as well."

"We're way too fertile when we're young."

"And horny," Veronica gasped.

We laughed from our bellies as the guys gave us weird looks.

"It's just girl talk. It's gossip."

"Yeah don't worry about it, you sexy BBQ men."

I don't think Lawrence classifies as sexy by any stretch of the imagination.

"I have to admit that I'd love a house like this."

"Of course you would. Everyone wants this house. You're all jealous of my life."

"Your blog is getting very popular."

"*Veronica's Vices.* It's all in the name. Plus, people love hearing about my lifestyle. They love to lust over the things they know they'll never have."

"At least you're humble."

"Oh, screw that. Lawrence says humble men end up in the dirt with nothing while men like him end up in the sky with millions."

"In the sky?" I asked.

"Yeah, something like that."

Veronica usually tried to say things that sounded deep, but actually weren't. It perfectly captured who she was as a person. She was all glitz and glamor on the outside. On the inside, she was as hollow as they came.

The food was ready, and the men served us plates then joined us. We shouted at the kids that lunch was being served but they didn't care. They wanted to keep playing. We would always let them have their fun.

"I am so happy our boys are best friends just like us."

"Thank god huh? Can you imagine if they weren't?"

"Oh, heavens no. Henry says it himself, they're are brothers on the court."

"That's what sports does to these young kids. It gives them so much passion. The guys on the team all love each other like family."

"The parents have a lot of passion too at the games," Veronica winked at Felix.

"I know, I know. I scream and yell. I can't help it. Henry makes incredible plays. I don't know how he does it. He's a beast!" Felix praised.

"Ethan also plays really good," I said nudging him.

"Yeah, of course. Ethan's great."

"You can't forget about our son, honey."

"I know, Sonya. Don't start please."

I stayed quiet and raised my eyebrows at Veronica. She awkwardly smiled. Lawrence remained an ice cube.

"Why don't we talk about Omar Pierce, hmm?"

"What about him?"

"You two are friends, no?"

"We are. He's my buddy," Felix said.

"He's been recently working at the school a lot, right?" Veronica asked.

"Yeah they've been transferring us in and out."

"Sonya tells me he helps a lot in her classroom."

"What? What is she talking about, honey?"

"Oh, it's nothing. He gives important lectures about safety, drunk driving, and the occasional police chase story. The kids love him. That's why he comes by."

"The kids aren't the only ones who love him," Veronica giggled.

"Why are you laughing? What are you implying?" Felix asked.

"No, nothing. Nothing at all," Veronica said as she took a swig of her drink.

"Don't listen to her, Felix. She's teasing you," I rolled my eyes.

"Is she?" Felix asked.

"Are you seriously asking me that?" I asked.

"Felix, you can't get jealous! Omar is a sexy piece of dark chocolatey goodness. It would be selfish not to let Sonya have a bite," Veronica said with a cheeky smile.

"Honey that is not appropriate," Lawrence coldly stated.

"People say our relationship isn't appropriate, but that didn't stop us," Veronica said.

"My apologies, folks. She is clearly drunk," Lawrence said.

"I'm not drunk. I'm just having a good time."

"For you, that usually means the same thing," Lawrence shot back.

"I'm gonna get another beer," Felix rose up and sped inside.

He definitely didn't appreciate Veronica's snarky comments.

"Daddy, where are you going?" Santi asked.

"Dad are you leaving?" Ethan asked.

He glanced at them and ignored them both.

"What? Oh my *god*, is he upset? I was just *joking*. We're having a *great* time aren't we?" Veronica slurred.

"I'll go talk to him," I said as I followed him inside.

I spotted him downing a beer in the living room while he sat on the couch and stared at the floor. I joined him and put my hand on his chest.

"Hey, what's wrong?" I asked.

"Why is Veronica saying all that stuff about Omar? Is something going on?" Felix asked.

"Seriously? You don't trust me?" I asked.

"I do, but why is she saying that stuff?" Felix asked.

"She's joking, honey. She's drunk."

"Do you like Omar? I mean, I get it. He's tall, handsome, and muscular. What's not to like? Sometimes I wanna punch the guy in the jaw and see if he's invincible too."

"No, I don't like him like that. He's just a friend. I love you, honey. You're my husband after all."

"Yeah?"

"Yeah."

"I'm sorry honey."

"It's okay."

"Omar hasn't tried anything has he? You know I can kick his ass right? It doesn't matter if he's bigger and stronger. I know kung-fu. I've watched a lot of YouTube."

"No, he's very respectful. I promise you."

"Okay. I believe you."

"Thank you."

"I love you, Sonya. I really do. I'm so happy you're my wife," Felix whispered as he wrapped his arms around me and planted a deep, warm kiss on my lips. I happily received it and smiled so wide, my mouth hurt.

"I love it when you kiss me like that."

"I love it too," Felix smiled.

"You know I'd never cheat on you, right?"

"I know," Felix replied as we continued kissing and forgot about our hosts outside.

That was the last happy memory I had with Felix and Veronica. I should've taken it as a sign that Felix didn't say he'd never cheat on me. I should've known, but one never does until it happens and that's the most tragic thing of all. It hits you like a car going 100 miles per hour and leaves an open wound so deep it never fully heals.

I was having a great day at work. Omar had actually swung by that day and was telling us a ridiculous story of the time he went on a wild goose chase to find an old lady's husband around her neighborhood. It was after four hours that he realized the old lady was a bit absent-minded and that her husband had been dead for 10 years. I left my classroom laughing to myself when Willow called me into her office. I had a habit of recalling past funny moments and giggling to myself like a lunatic.

Willow looked uncharacteristically grim when I walked in and sat down across from her. She was sitting at her desk and had her phone in her hand.

"Hi Sonya," Willow said.

"Hey, what's up?" I asked.

Willow became misty-eyed as she opened her mouth and struggled to find the words. I got up and gripped her arm.

"What's wrong? Did something happen? Are you okay?" I asked.

"I'm okay. Well, not really because I'm about to show you something that's going to make you very upset and that's gonna make me very upset," Willow admitted.

"What is it?" I asked.

I had no idea what she was about to show me. I wished I hadn't been so naïve.

"It's better if you see it for yourself," Willow said.

She raised her phone and showed me the screen. There was a paused video. She pressed play. It was a bit dark and grainy, but you could make out what was happening. There was two people kissing and having sex in a car. It looked like a police car. When it zoomed in, I gasped. It was Felix and Veronica. They were having sex. Together. The two of them. My husband and my best friend. Soon to be ex-husband and ex-best-friend.

I immediately collapsed to the floor and had trouble breathing as my chest felt like it was caving in on itself. The crying came fast and heavy. My entire face was a mess of tears, snot and anguish as my marriage was shattered before my very eyes. Willow came down to the floor with me and held me tight as I let out my pain and sorrow in the form of muffled screams. I bawled for what felt like hours until I finally ran out of tears and felt nothing but a deep emptiness. I remained on the floor and stared into space as I slowly realized what the end of my marriage meant for my children and myself.

Dark times are coming.

"I'm so, so sorry, Sonya. I'm so sorry. Maybe I shouldn't have shown you the video. God, I'm such an idiot. I'm a stupid idiot."

"No, Willow. It's okay. I needed to see. I needed to see how they betrayed me."

"I found them in the parking lot, Sonya. They have no shame. I hate them both."

"I hate them so much I could kill them both. I could seriously murder them both."

I shocked myself when I said that. I knew I wasn't readily capable of murder, but given the right set of circumstances...who knew?

"Who knows how long it's been going."

"What are you gonna do now?"

"I'm gonna confront him."

"Tonight?"

"I'm gonna check his computer and his work phone while he goes on his run," I said.

"He has a work phone? Oh god," Willow gasped.

"I thought he barely used it because I never saw him with it. Now, I know why," I said.

"My god, Sonya. This is so horrible. I never thought Felix would do something like this."

"The Felix I met would've never cheated on me, but something happened halfway through our marriage. It was like he gave up. He didn't care anymore. I thought we had made good progress recently, getting to the place we used to be in, in the beginning. Clearly, I was dead wrong."

"What about the kids? Are you gonna tell them?" Willow asked.

"Absolutely not. Not right now. They can't know. They'll know when they're older."

"I hope they turn out okay. I hope *you* are okay. I know this'll take time to get over but I'm always here for you."

"You're a great friend, Willow. Thank you," I choked out.

During the nightmare with Ethan, I often wondered if he would be in the terrible situation he was in if Felix hadn't cheated. I couldn't pinpoint why but it felt like things would be different. Perhaps if Felix was a decent father he would've been able to protect Ethan and prevent him from being arrested. I don't know. One thing was for sure though, Felix had a major part to play in causing ruin in our lives. I wasn't going to stand by and let myself be a victim, but Felix was a bastard for what he did to our family. Despite that, I was a survivor. I did what I had to do to go on. I had to continue to live on for myself and for my children.

When I arrived later that night at my house, I felt like a ghost floating through the wind. I saw Felix in the kitchen, wearing his athletic gear. He was prepping for his night run and filling up his water bottle. I wanted to snatch it out of his hands, throw the water in his face and beat his head in with the metallic bottle until he fell unconscious. He glanced at me and grinned. I reluctantly reciprocated.

"I'm going for my run, honey. I'll see you in an hour."

"Okay," I replied.

As soon as he left I jetted up the stairs and made sure the kids were asleep. Once that was confirmed I went into our bedroom and got on his laptop.

One hour.

I quickly scrolled through all his files, emails, Skype conversations and didn't find anything even remotely suspicious. I cursed under my breath. I started rummaging through all of his things. I didn't care anymore. I turned that room upside down, trying to find his work phone. I emptied out his drawers, I tossed the belongings he had on his side of the closet to the ground, I turned his nightstand upside down and allowed everything to fall on the floor. A bunch of condoms, coins, headphones, and wristbands fell out.

Look at all these condoms. We're only having sex once a month.

I lifted up his side of the bed and saw a square hole that was cut into the mattress. I had seen it before, but Felix told me that it was his hiding spot for his emergency gun and to never touch it.

Excellent cover story.

I reached inside and took out a metal box. It had a lock with a 4-digit code. He was never good with passwords. I used the same one he had for his laptop and unlatched it. There was a handgun inside as well as a phone.

It wasn't his personal one, so I knew I had found it. I looked at the gun and considered grabbing it for a split-second. I took out the phone, locked the box back up and placed it back in its hiding spot. He didn't even bother to have a passcode. That's how sure he was I'd never find it. It boiled my blood. I was livid.

I went directly to his photo album and saw everything I needed to see. An entire gallery of nude photos of Veronica and Felix. Felix even had nude pictures of a few other girls I didn't recognize. He was a sick, selfish bastard. I hated him with every fiber of my being. I wanted him dead. If it weren't for my children, I'd take his gun and shoot him in the head as soon as he walked in the door. I'd gladly go to prison if I knew he was gone from the world forever.

I went to his text messages and read the conversations he had with Veronica. It was nothing but sexually charged messages and sweet nothings being exchanged back and forth. They sent photos, talked dirty and planned secret locations for hooking up. I felt like I was gonna throw up. I sat down on my bed and shuddered.

I couldn't believe that it was all there. The complete and ultimate betrayal of not only my husband but my supposed best friend. I had known both for about 10 years. 10 years of marriage and friendship down the drain. It was one of the most painful experiences of my entire life. I cried every night for months afterwards. It had been too much to bear in the beginning.

I heard Felix jogging up the stairs. I suddenly grew anxious, but I prepared myself to confront him. I stood up and held his *work* phone in my hand. He entered, sweaty and jamming out to the music on his headphones. He saw me glaring at him and took off his headphones.

"Something wrong, beautiful?" Felix asked.

He noticed all his things on the floor and threw his hands up in the air.

"What the hell is going on?"

"How long?" I asked shakily.

"What? Why is all my stuff everywhere? Are you doing another one of your deep cleanings right now? It's bedtime, Sonya. Your husband needs his beauty sleep."

"How long have you been sleeping with Veronica?"

Felix turned white and hesitated.

"I— I don't know what you're talking about." Felix turned away.

"Don't even try that bullshit with me, Felix. Do not even try it!" I shouted.

"Keep your damn voice down. The kids are asleep."

"Answer my question before I lose it."

"You've already lost it, lady. I need to shower."

"Hey, *fuck you*. I know that you've been cheating on me, and I want you to fucking admit it, you piece of shit."

"I really don't know what you're talking about, Sonya.".

I threw his work phone at him, and he barely caught it.

"Explain all that then. Nice pictures by the way," I hissed.

"Where did you get this?"

"Does it matter?"

"Why are you going through my things?"

"Answer my damn question, Felix."

"I don't understand why you're going through my things."

"I don't understand why you've been cheating on me with my best friend."

"You weren't supposed to find this," Felix sighed.

"Yeah, no shit," I snapped.

"She told you, didn't she? She felt guilty. Is that it?"

"No, she didn't. Someone saw you two idiots having sex in your police car. Genius plan."

"Oh, that. I'm sorry, but you need to understand that she came on to me first," Felix pleaded.

"I don't care what your stupid excuses are. You need to answer my question. How long have you been sleeping with her?"

"It's been about a year, Sonya. Jesus, why would you ask me that?" Felix asked.

"*A fucking year,*" I choked out.

"I messed up. I'm sorry."

"No, no, no, no, no. There's no coming back from this. Our marriage is over."

"Now wait a second. What the hell are you talking about? Don't say that."

"You cheated on me, it's over. You betrayed everything we had together."

"I can fix things, Sonya. We can talk this through. We can work on it," Felix pleaded.

"There's nothing to talk about you idiot. It's over. It wasn't a onetime thing. You had sex with her for a year. A whole year. You're disgusting. The both of you are dead to me."

"It meant nothing to me. I don't love her."

"It's over. There's absolutely nothing you can say that can change my mind," I said sternly.

"What about the kids? Huh? What about them? You're gonna make things confusing for them."

"Who's fault is that?"

"You're such an annoying bitch," Felix hissed.

"Right, of course I'm the bitch. Don't pretend to love the kids, Felix. You barely talk to them."

"Hey, I love my kids. I work a lot, okay? I'm sorry that I need my alone time. What the hell is the matter with you?"

"Your alone time consisted of you sneaking away to have sex with Veronica. You're a fucking clown, Felix," I thundered.

"I'm not a clown. I'm your husband."

"You're a real piece of shit. I wish I realized that before I married you," I shot back.

"We're not getting a divorce," Felix threatened.

"Yes we are."

"No."

"I'm not forgiving you in this lifetime or in the next for what you did, you need to accept that."

Felix rushed towards me and violently grabbed my arm. He looked at me with rage-filled, bloodshot eyes as my heart started racing.

"What are you doing? You're hurting me."

"If I say we're not getting a divorce, we're not getting one. Okay?" Felix asked.

"I'm not your property, you asshole. Let go of me!" I yelled as I pushed him off. Felix's rage overtook him, and he backhanded me so hard across the face I fell to the floor. I immediately shielded my face with my hands and crawled back to the wall. Felix's expression softened when he realized what he had done. He almost looked remorseful. He took a knee and held out his hand.

"Jesus, Sonya. I'm sorry. I don't know what got into me. You just get me so mad sometimes that I can't control it. I love you, Sonya. I love you so much. What happened between me, and Veronica doesn't mean anything. I swear to you. You're the only woman I love."

"I want a *fucking* divorce," I said forcefully.

Felix didn't like how that sounded. He immediately grew angry again and sprang back up. He raced towards the bed, lifted it, and took out the metal box. I feared the worst as he unlocked it and pulled out his gun. He catapulted himself onto me and shoved the gun inside my mouth. I froze as I felt the ice cold barrel on my tongue. Dozens of sweat droplets were dripping down my face as my heart felt like it was about to implode from how fast it was beating.

"Think about the kids. Think about Ethan and Santi not having a mother. Please," I whispered.

"I hate you, Sonya. I *hate* you."

"Please don't kill me, Felix. Please don't do it. You'll destroy your life. You'll destroy Ethan's life. You'll destroy Santi's life. You'll destroy mine," I softly pleaded.

He put his finger on the trigger for a few minutes as he slowly breathed in and out. It felt like an eternity. It felt like it was the end for me. I would die a victim of domestic violence. Everything was over. My life was done. I was done being a teacher, a mother, a daughter, a wife, and a friend. I closed my eyes and waited to enter the darkness.

To my shock, he took the gun out of my mouth, and I heard him storm out of the room. I buried my face in my hands and silently sobbed. I was alive. I had been spared, but in a way my life was still over.

I had to start again. My marriage crumbled before my very eyes and my decade-long friendship with someone I considered a sister was erased in the span of a day. I was officially a single woman again. I had to begin again during a tragic event in my childhood. Now I had to do it yet again.

I was prepared for it. I knew what to expect and I knew what I had to do. I had to stay strong and steady through it all. If you allowed yourself to stay in that dark place for long, you would lose yourself forever. I knew it couldn't happen. I wouldn't allow myself to lose who I was.

A short while later, I felt two small bodies wrapping themselves around me. I glanced up and saw my Ethan and Santi hugging me. I brought them in closer and quietly apologized for everything that had happened.

"We love you mom," Ethan and Santi repeated until we fell asleep together.

We all lie to save ourselves.

CHAPTER 9
PRESENT DAY

While I graded papers in my classroom during my free period, I overheard students talking in the hallway.

You heard? Someone from Skyview was released from jail.

Who do you think it is?

Bro it might be Ethan.

This is gonna be crazy.

I immediately called Omar, but he wasn't answering, so I shot up and went straight to Willow's office. I scrolled through social media to try and find a name but saw nothing. They were keeping the person anonymous. I barged in on her while she was on a phone call. I waited until she was done.

"You always come at the best times," Willow said as she hung up the phone.

"Is it true? A student has been released from custody?" I asked.

"Yes, but it's not Ethan. I'm sorry," Willow offered.

"Who got released then?" I asked.

"Jonathan Locke, the basketball player. The student who pretty much accused your son of murdering Henry." Willow reminded me.

"I remember."

"Are you planning on doing something?" Willow asked.

"No."

"Are you lying to me?"

"Yes."

"Just don't accuse him of being a pedophile please," Willow pleaded.

"I'll keep it civil." I promised.

"You better."

After school I caught up to Jonathan in the gym before basketball practice started. He was startled when I tapped him on the shoulder, and he looked like he wanted to run. I offered him a friendly smile so he wouldn't bolt.

"I come in peace, Jonathan. I heard you were just released from jail?" I asked.

"I was, yeah," Jonathan said cautiously.

"How was it?"

"It sucked balls," Jonathan admitted.

"Right, that's obvious."

"Am I in trouble?" Jonathan asked.

"No, of course not. I just wanted to ask you why you were yelling out that Ethan had something to do with Henry's disappearance on the day you were arrested. That's all."

Jonathan looked like I had just gut-punched him and sucked out all the air from his lungs.

"I don't know. I was saying anything. I didn't wanna get arrested."

"I promise that you're not in trouble. You can tell me, Jonathan."

"Alright look, they were best friends once, but I think they started to secretly hate each other after a while. I don't think they've liked each other for years now," Jonathan confessed.

"Why would you say that?" I asked.

"Ethan hated the fact that Henry always started over him on the team and that he always got more minutes. Henry would also rub it in his face a lot in the locker room. I don't know. They used to say they were brothers or whatever but I wasn't seeing that. What I saw was two guys who couldn't stand each other anymore. Ethan was jealous of Henry and Henry did everything he could to make that worse."

I was beginning to seriously understand why Ethan had a motive to hate and murder Henry. It shook me to my very core. I grew ever more afraid for Ethan. I knew there was things he wasn't telling me, and I wasn't sure what to think anymore. All signs pointed towards Ethan murdering Henry that fateful night…but he was my son. Could I ever go against my own child? Doubt him? Fear him?

"What about Layla? Did Ethan hate Henry because of what he was doing to her?" I asked.

"It's obvious Henry had a little crush on her, but she's Ethan's girl. There was nothing he could do about that."

"Did you ever see Henry do inappropriate things with Layla behind my son's back?" I asked.

Jonathan darted his eyes around me, refusing to meet my steady gaze. He swallowed hard.

"No."

It sounded like someone was trying to protect his dead friend's name.

"How close were you with Henry?" I asked.

"Honestly Ms. Salvador, Henry was my boy for life. I loved that kid. He was one of the good ones for sure. He always tried to work things out with Ethan in the end, you know? Henry was like that. I know he's your son and all, but I'm not sure Ethan wanted the same thing. It was a complicated brotherhood," Jonathan admitted.

It sounded like Jonathan was *Team Henry*. I wondered how many teammates actually supported Ethan. I hadn't seen many online posts that supported Ethan. What I saw were countless posts dedicated to Henry's life, his high school basketball career, and compilations of videos that his friends had taken with him before he was murdered. Was Ethan jealous of Henry's life? Was he angry that Henry wanted to take Layla from him? Did that tip him over the edge? Was I overthinking things?

"I just have one more question and I'll get out of your hair," I said.

"Go ahead."

The explosive question that's been on my mind since I heard you were released.

"Is it true you placed a bloodied box cutter in my son's locker?" I asked.

"What box cutter?" Jonathan asked.

"The one you were in possession of."

"Uh, what? No, no I didn't. I didn't even touch your son's locker," Jonathan stuttered.

"Don't lie to me," I demanded.

Jonathan took a few steps back.

"How did you know about that? Only the cops should know about that," Jonathan mumbled.

"All you need to worry about is answering the question," I urged.

"I was just trying to protect someone. I swear," Jonathan pleaded.

"Who?" I asked.

"You wouldn't understand. None of you understand," Jonathan muttered.

"You can talk to me. I'd understand. I'm a teacher, you can trust me. What's going on, Jonathan?" I asked.

"No, you wouldn't get it. The police wouldn't either. Are you undercover or something? Why are you asking me so many questions? Are you trying to get me arrested again?" Jonathan asked.

"No, of course not. Please, don't shut yourself off. I just want to know the truth. I need to help my son."

"Screw your son. You think you know him, but you don't. You don't know the things he's capable of. He murdered my boy, Henry. You need to accept that. Ethan *murdered* Henry!" Jonathan shouted as he ran off.

"Jonathan, wait!" I pleaded.

He ignored me as the rest of the team started piling in and giving me curious looks. They cheered and celebrated Jonathan's return by hoisting him up. I smiled in their direction and got a couple of friendly waves, but the rest of the team stared at me like I was some hideous monster. I guessed that Ethan wasn't as popular as I thought. I got out of there before Coach Albert showed up. I wasn't interested in him questioning me. Jonathan would undoubtedly rat me out.

I walked to the front of the school and saw Omar's police cruiser parked. I went over and knocked on the window. He promptly unlocked the door, and I slid in. He was typing on a module-like computer and was listening to the police radio.

"You know you can't really be in my car unless you're sitting in the back right?" Omar asked.

"Yeah, well, I'm not being arrested for anything am I?"

"I'm sorry I've been dodging your calls. It's been getting really busy with this case."

"I've noticed. You guys released Jonathan Locke even though you have footage of him placing an alleged murder weapon inside my son's locker."

"I don't know why they released him. They're keeping that very quiet. There's something else going on."

"What are you talking about?"

"I've been trying to find out what the deal is with Jonathan, but I'm getting shut out. There's another police unit involved now."

"Does this have to do with Henry's murder?"

"Maybe, maybe not. I'd go with yes because everything has to do with Henry's murder right now. We have Lawrence and Veronica calling the station 24/7 demanding answers. Lawrence has been running ads online through his media companies targeting us for being incompetent and slow. Veronica has been bad-mouthing us nonstop on her dumb blog, *Veronica's Vices*. It's been a real shit show."

"Why don't you get them to stop?"

"It's very simple, they're very rich. Lawrence has influence, a good relationship with Chief Delatorre and he donates a lot of money to the police department."

"Of course he does."

"There should be news about your son soon. The lab results from the DNA tests are due any minute now."

I gripped Omar's hand, much to his surprise. We met each other's eyes.

"Thank you, Omar, for everything."

"I got your back."

"I got yours too."

"I really hope my son turns out okay. He's too young for all this. He's too young for his life to be destroyed forever."

"Do you think he murdered Henry Cain?"

The truth was, I wasn't so sure anymore. I didn't know what to think or what to believe. All I knew was that I wanted him free, I wanted him home and I desperately wanted everything to go back to normal.

"No."

"I don't think so either. He'll be fine."

Santi was quiet again on the car ride. We were on route to Felix's house.

"Are you okay, Santi?" I asked.

"Yeah," Santi mumbled.

"Are you still shaken up about the other night?" I asked.

"Yeah."

"It's okay, sweetie. I get it. It won't happen again," I promised.

"Did Omar arrest them?" Santi asked.

"No because the police don't know who did it. We don't know either so there's not much we can do about it. We have to move on and keep our heads up. Okay?" I asked.

"Okay mom."

"Are they still bullying you about Ethan?" I asked.

"They won't shut up about it, mom. I try ignoring them, but random kids keep screaming at me when I'm walking in the halls. I don't even see who it is."

"What are they screaming?" I asked.

"That Ethan is a bloody murderer and that he should die next. That's the gist of it."

I furiously shook my head.

"My god, these kids are something else."

"Even dad says that Ethan killed him," Santi revealed.

I froze for a second and repeated what Santi had said in my mind.

"Excuse me?" I asked.

"When is Ethan coming home?" Santi asked.

"I don't know, sweetheart. I wish I did." I said.

"Is he ever coming home?" Santi asked.

It was a tough question. He had to come home. There was no way he wouldn't. But I had to be prepared for the possibility that he didn't. I couldn't lose myself. I had to stay tough for Santi.

"He will, Santi. He'll come home soon," I said.

Santi stayed quiet and turned away for the rest of the ride. I was absolutely simmering by the time we got to Felix's house. I sent him to his room and practically pulled out Felix by his ear.

"Christ almighty, Sonya. What is it now? I was getting my drink on," Felix said.

"So sorry to interrupt you getting your *drink on*, but why are you telling Santi that Ethan murdered Henry? Do you want to explain that to me before I go berserk?"

"You are a very bad-tempered woman. You know that?" Felix asked.

"People like you make me that way."

"Well, you were never the charmer. I had to be," Felix smirked.

"I don't give a shit, Felix. We're not even talking about that. Why are you telling Santi that his brother killed Henry?" I asked.

"It's time to be realistic, Sonya. Look at all the facts and the evidence. He had the alleged murder weapon in his locker, he had his blood on his hands, they fought physically, and they had a history of hating each other. Lord knows what they'll find on his phone," Felix said.

"I'm glad to see you support your own blood," I said.

"I'm trying to prepare Santi for the inevitable news, Sonya. Something you're unwilling to do," Felix said.

"I'm sorry that I believe that my son is innocent and I'm sorry that you don't."

"Whatever, Sonya."

"You know they didn't hate each other. They were best friends for a long time. I don't know what happened during the end, but I don't think it would be so terrible that it would lead to Ethan murdering him. That is absolutely unthinkable," I said.

On the outside I was Ethan's number one supporter and protector. On the inside, thoughts of doubt surrounding the evidence stacked against him plagued my mind. I tried my best to shut them out.

"I've been a police officer for a very long time, Sonya. I've worked in high schools for a lot of that time. Trust me when I say that you don't know what teenagers are fully capable of. I've seen stabbings, shootings, kids getting their brains smashed in with a textbook, kids getting thrown down the stairs and a kid getting choked out with a shoelace because he took someone else's favorite seat during lunchtime. Ethan slashing Henry's throat isn't that farfetched."

"I've been a high school teacher for a long time too. I know what happens," I said.

"Good, so you understand that we need to tell Santi the truth when it's time," Felix said.

"What truth? You are a lunatic! He hasn't even been charged with anything. I called Arthur Faraday, and he confirmed it himself," I said.

"I don't care about Arthur Faraday."

Trying to have a discussion with Felix was like arguing with a 5-year-old.

"Are you even on Ethan's side?" I asked.

"I'm looking at the reality of the situation, Sonya," Felix groaned.

"No, you know what I think? I think you loved Henry more than you love your own son."

"That's not true."

"You're still in love with Veronica too. Right?" I asked.

Felix scoffed and shook his head.

"What do you want me to say?" Felix asked.

"You're pathetic," I whispered.

"I'm sorry that I still love her. Is that what you wanna hear? I'm so sorry that I slept with your best friend and that I am still madly in love with her," Felix said.

"You're mentally ill."

"Baby, if being in love is an illness, call me fucking crazy," Felix mocked.

"Stop telling our son that Ethan is a murderer please. I'm trying my best to keep him calm. You're not helping by saying that stupid shit," I said as I stomped back to my car.

"You get mad when I don't talk to him, and you get mad when I do talk to him. What the hell do you want from me, lady?" Felix asked.

I was married to him for ten years. I only had myself to blame. When I went to sleep that night, I had the nightmare again. Sometimes it changed, sometimes it stayed the same. I was in a dark room on the second floor of a decrepit house. The wooden floor was ice cold. Two people towered over me. One was an older man and the other was an older woman. They looked like a married couple. The darkness of the room hid their faces. They were having a volcanic argument about something I didn't understand. The man savagely punched the woman in the stomach which caused her to double-over and cough up blood. He then kicked her down to the ground as she yelped in pain. I tried to move my feet, but they were stuck in place like quicksand. It ended with the man menacingly coming towards me.

I woke up in a cold sweat to a phone call. It was Arthur Faraday. I swiftly answered.

"Sonya, your son has been released. I need you down at the station immediately."

Without a moment's hesitation, I got dressed, raced down to my car, and sped down the street.

CHAPTER 10

There were several news vans and reporters clamoring to get a word out of Ethan as Arthur and Omar tried their best to push them aside.

Will Ethan Salvador be charged?!

Did Ethan murder Henry Cain?!

Has the murder weapon been recovered?!

Is it true you were best friends with Henry?!

Ethan, why did you murder your friend and teammate?!

Ethan stopped and glared at the reporter who asked that question. They all became quiet at once, hysterically eager for his response.

"I didn't kill anyone. Henry was my best friend."

They continued shouting out questions which caused Ethan to grow visibly irritated.

"Please! Hello! No more questions at this time," Arthur said.

They didn't listen to him. Omar and a couple of other officers attempted to hold back the relentless mob as Ethan ran into my arms. I warmly embraced him for several minutes as tears of joy ran down my cheek. I kissed his head and refused to let go.

"I'm so happy you're out, baby. You don't know how worried I was. They wouldn't even let me visit you."

"I'm okay, mom. I'm okay. I'm out now."

"Did they treat you okay? Did they hurt you?" I asked.

"It was whatever. They didn't hurt me."

"You're not lying to me, are you?"

"No, mom. I swear."

"Okay, sweetie. Let's go home before this mob tramples us."

"I'm hungry. Can we get some food?"

"What do you want?" I asked.

"Anything," Ethan said.

Once we got home, Ethan ate a full course dinner complete with garlic mashed potatoes, creamy mac and cheese, flaky biscuits, and grilled chicken from a local BBQ restaurant. After he devoured his 10-pound meal, he immediately hit the shower. I was downstairs with Santi, watching him do his homework.

"When is he coming down?" Santi asked.

"He's taking a much-needed shower. He'll be down soon."

"You promise?" Santi asked.

"Yes, of course."

"Why didn't he say hi to me when he came?" Santi asked.

"You were taking a nap."

"You should've woke me up."

I appreciated the love my boys had for each other. Sometimes it felt like it was just the two of them against the world. Almost everyone had turned against Ethan while he was in police custody. Nasty ads and online posts made by Lawrence's media companies were targeting Ethan and the circumstantial evidence that was stacked against him. They had pictures of his mugshot plastered over a black wall and branded him, **MURDERER**, in bright red letters.

It infuriated me. They argued that since he apparently had Henry's blood on his hands and the alleged murder weapon in his locker, he was Henry's murderer. Every detail about the case that was supposed to be confidential was being leaked. I figured it was Felix being an ass, but I couldn't say for sure.

They also had the video of him fighting Henry across all social media sites. The headline read: *Ethan beat Henry within an inch of his life just days before his murder. Did he decide to finish the job?*

The more I watched the video, the more it horrified me. It was clear that Ethan had done the most damage. You could see him whacking him on the nose causing the blood to spill on Ethan's hand. My question was why did Ethan still have traces of his blood, days later? Maybe I just didn't understand how long blood could stay on someone's skin. Ethan came down to the living room with a towel wrapped around his wet hair. He was wearing a pink robe and fluffy slippers.

"Is that my robe?" I asked.

"I think pink is my color, mom. I hope you don't mind."

"Only this time," I smirked.

"Bro!" Santi shouted as he ran towards Ethan and gave him a tight hug.

"Careful man, I don't want the robe to slip. You'll be seeing things you should never see."

"Why didn't you wake me up from my nap?" Santi asked.

"You looked peaceful. I thought about farting on you, but I decided to be nice. I'm out of jail now. I'm trying to be a better person."

"You're still dumb," Santi said.

"And you're still a butthead," Ethan replied.

"I'm really happy you're back, bro."

"Me too, man. I'll never take a warm shower for granted again."

"It was that bad?"

"Toilet seat was ice cold; food was shit and the people were either really scary or really weird. It was a messed-up experience. I'm never going back there. I can't. I'll go insane," Ethan said.

"That was just a holding cell too. Imagine an actual prison and being there for years," I said.

"I'd lose my mind. I'd miss you guys too much and Layla. Oh my god, Layla. I gotta call her. I'll be back," Ethan ran off.

"So do you know why they decided to let him go?" Santi asked.

"I'm not sure, everything has been such a whirlwind. The lawyer's coming by later to explain everything he knows," I said.

"Can I listen to that?" Santi asked.

"No, you need to go to bed. You still have school tomorrow."

After I sent Santi to bed, Arthur arrived 20 minutes later. Ethan came back from his phone call, and we gathered around to talk things through.

"How was Layla?" I asked.

"She's really happy I'm out. She was crying. I'll see her tomorrow," Ethan said.

"Good," I said, while putting my arm around him and pulling him in.

"First of all, we're so happy that you're out, Ethan. I know you've been through a very tough ordeal, but you've pulled through. You're out and that's all that matters now," Arthur said.

"Thank you Arthur. You've been incredibly helpful," I said.

"Yes, thank you sir," Ethan said.

"I'm happy to be of service. Now, onto the important details surrounding your release. You were released because they deemed there was insufficient evidence, lack of witnesses and other variables that didn't justify officially charging you with Henry's murder after your 72-hour hold. Your alibi turned out to be solid enough it seems. Your mother and Layla did both vouch for you after all. They didn't find anything incriminating on your phone, which is a huge plus. There's a short press conference that will be held tomorrow morning announcing your release and the reasoning behind that decision. Ethan, bottom line is that the blood that they tested from your hands came back as inconclusive. They can't decipher if it came from Henry or not," Arthur explained.

"Holy shit," Ethan cursed.

"If those test results came back positive for Henry's DNA, we might've been talking through a jail cell by now," Arthur admitted.

"We caught a lucky break then," I breathed.

"One thing that worries me is that the test results from the bloodied box cutter found in your locker has not been released yet," Arthur said.

"What do you think that means?" I asked.

"Well that could mean that it's simply not ready yet. Which would be odd given the timeframe. It could also mean the blood belongs to someone else," Arthur said.

"Oh my god. Could that be true?" I asked.

"That would be nuts. I still can't believe someone put that box cutter in my locker. Someone's trying to frame me, mom."

"I figured, honey," I said.

"Did they find out who it was?" Ethan asked.

"Well, yes," I said.

"Who?" Ethan asked.

"It was Jonathan Locke."

"Jonathan?! Are you serious? That snake. Why would he do that?"

"I have no idea."

"To be honest with you, I thought Jonathan Locke was going to be the primary suspect in Henry's murder, but they released him earlier so I'm at a loss. I fear they might want to gather all the evidence they can, arrest Ethan again and go full force when the test results of the box cutter's blood is released," Arthur said.

"No way," Ethan muttered.

"Can they do that?" I asked.

"They can arrest a suspect multiple times within reason," Arthur said.

"What if the blood on the box cutter belongs to someone else?" Ethan asked.

"Frankly, I have no idea. It would depend on the DNA they find and who it would belong to. Jonathan placed it in your locker so naturally he would be arrested, but it's very strange he's been released. We'll have to wait and see what the police do," Arthur said.

"They still think it's me, don't they? This is stupid. I didn't do it!" Ethan punched the side of the couch.

"Try to calm down, son. It'll be okay," Arthur said.

"Ethan don't lose your cool. We'll get through this together," I promised.

"If they try to arrest me again, I'll steal one of their guns and shoot my way out to escape. It'll be like *Grand Theft Auto*."

I stared at him in horror as he chuckled.

"I strongly urge you not to steal a car. Grand theft auto is a very serious offense and would not help your case whatsoever," Arthur said.

"He didn't mean it, Arthur. It's a silly video game," I said.

"Oh. Well, you lost me there," Arthur said as he stood up.

"Thank you so much for everything," I said.

"It's my pleasure to represent the innocent. Ethan, I would stay off the internet if I were you and I would not pay attention to Lawrence

Whitlock's smear campaigns. They're very distasteful," Arthur said as I walked him out.

"What campaigns?" Ethan asked.

"Lawrence has been putting out some ads stating that you're Henry's murderer," I said.

"Lawrence as in Henry's dad? Is he insane?" Ethan asked.

"He wants justice for his dead son. I understand him, but that isn't the way to do it," I said.

"I can't even imagine the forums online. There must be a million conspiracy theories on why I killed him. So stupid," Ethan snapped.

"What's important is that you didn't kill him."

"Am I going to school tomorrow?"

"No, you can take it easy for a few days. I have assignments from your teachers."

"Oh, great. More useless schoolwork. Maybe it wouldn't be so bad going back to jail," Ethan scoffed.

I playfully hit his shoulder.

"Don't even joke like that," I said.

"Mom, what color was the box cutter found in my locker?" Ethan asked.

"I'm pretty sure it was black, why?" I asked.

"Black? Holy shit. That's Griffin's box cutter," Ethan said.

My heart pounded as I heard that name coming out of Ethan's mouth.

Griffin. He has to be the one. I knew he was suspicious, I thought.

"It is? Are you sure?" I asked.

"I'm positive. It has his initials inscribed on it. The police should've noticed that by now," Ethan said.

"Maybe they know something we don't."

"Maybe," Ethan said.

"How do you know it's his box cutter? Have you used it?" I asked.

"Yeah, he gets some of us to open up the boxes of textbooks he orders every year for every class. He gets like 4 different versions, all from different publishers. He's insane," Ethan said.

"Who's *some of us*?" I asked.

"The athletes who have him for class and some guys from the baseball team. He gives us extra credit. We're the only ones who know where he keeps it."

"So it's Mr. Griffin's box cutter and Jonathan put it in your locker."

"Do you know why Jonathan was arrested in the first place? I know he was a suspect, but why? He worshipped Henry. I don't see how he could be involved in Henry's murder." Ethan said.

"I don't know. I asked your father, and he didn't know. Omar hasn't told me anything either."

"It's so weird. Why would Mr. Griffin send Jonathan to put that box cutter in my locker?" Ethan asked aloud.

"Wait, how do you know that? Why would he send him to do that?"

"I don't know why or how he did it, but the one thing I do know is that Jonathan is scared of Mr. Griffin, and he isn't the only one."

CHAPTER 11

I stayed up all night thinking about what Ethan had told me. I thought up all the possibilities and probabilities in Henry's murder. I thought about the identity of his murderer and who it could actually be. I went over it in my head again and again and again. I was completely out of it the next day but at least I had avoided my recurring nightmare. There was only so many times I could stomach seeing that old man's body explode into blood and concrete dust.

I made urgent calls to Willow and Omar. I needed to meet with them in Willow's office immediately. There was a lot to discuss.

"I'm happy your son is out, Sonya," Omar said.

"Me too."

"Finally. He shouldn't have been arrested in the first place," Willow glared at Omar.

"There was probable cause. The alleged murder weapon was found in his locker, among other things," Omar defended.

"Why was he released then? I'll tell you why because they know he's innocent," Willow snapped.

"There could be a few different reasons why, Willow. This is a very complicated case," Omar pleaded.

"It's not complicated, he didn't do it," Willow argued.

"You weren't there," Omar snapped.

"Obviously, I was at a meeting with prehistoric men. But, I do know Ethan would never do something like this."

"I need to know something before I give my theory," I interjected.

"What?" Omar asked.

"Why was Jonathan arrested?" I asked.

Omar shifted uncomfortably.

"I've already told you way more than I should have. You shouldn't be this involved in this case," Omar said.

"I already was from the very beginning. This is my son we're talking about. A teenager accused of murdering his best friend. This is as serious as it gets for a mother."

"Alright, this doesn't leave this room. I'm serious. I'm only saying this because you're a good friend," Omar demanded.

We both nodded.

"Jonathan was arrested because school resource officers saw him with blood on his hands and when they went to question him, he ran. The lab tested the blood and it matched Henry's DNA," Omar explained.

Our jaws dropped to the floor.

"Are you kidding me? So Jonathan murdered Henry?" I asked.

"We don't think so. He claimed he cut himself with the knife and his DNA also showed up as a match. It doesn't add up. We think the real murderer forced him to get rid of the murder weapon in Ethan's locker to pin it on him. We don't think he did it because he has a strong alibi. He was out with friends that night after practice and went to a local diner to have a late dinner. We were able to confirm with the staff that was working that night that he was there. They had camera footage and everything. You can't be at two places at once," Omar explained.

"He must've been really nervous to cut himself with that knife," I said.

"It's very sharp," Omar admitted.

"That's why he was released then. He simply couldn't have been there at the time of Henry's murder," Willow said.

"That's part of it. The detectives tried to get him to talk more but he was too afraid. We think he knows who killed Henry, but he won't say it because the murderer will go after him. He's absolutely terrified of this person. Whoever it is. We let him go because we wanted to trail him in hopes that he would go back to Henry's murderer. He hasn't yet, but we're optimistic," Omar said.

"You've been busy," I said.

"Like I said, this case has been complicated. I'm doing all I can to clear Ethan's good name and to find out who really murdered Henry. That's all I'm interested in," Omar said.

"I think my theory is plausible then. I believe Mr. Griffin killed Henry," I said.

"Whoa, Claude Griffin?" Omar asked.

"That's one hell of an accusation!" Willow exclaimed.

"I think Mr. Griffin murdered Henry because he threatened to out him as a sexual predator. Mr. Griffin then forced Jonathan to get rid of the murder weapon in Ethan's locker to pin it on him," I theorized.

"Why would he choose Ethan's locker?" Omar asked.

"He saw the leaked video of the fight between Ethan and Henry and hatched his plan," I said.

"That's not bad. That's not bad at all," Omar said.

"Jonathan also tried to pin suspicion on Ethan when he was being arrested," I said.

"Why would Jonathan be involved with Mr. Griffin like that?" Omar asked.

"He's afraid of him," I said.

"Mr. Griffin has a rumored history of sexually harassing, and abusing boys on the baseball team when he was head coach. No one ever apparently saw anything though, and no one ever spoke up so nothing could be done. All we could do was remove him as head coach. He's well-liked by my bosses because he led the baseball team to several state titles. They almost fired me when the athletic director and I removed him," Willow revealed.

"That's insane. Do you think he's a sexual predator?" Omar asked.

"I don't know. He's really nice to everyone but when I asked for anonymous votes from the student government to state whether or not they thought he was a predator, they all voted yes. I had to believe them."

"You seriously asked the student government?" Omar asked.

"I needed an answer from competent students. They're good, honest kids. I trust them."

"How did Mr. Griffin take it?" Omar asked.

"He seemed irked, but he took it pretty well. He's eligible in a couple of years to win back his position," Willow stated.

"You removed a man purely based on rumor and anonymous voting. That's interesting." Omar raised his eyebrows.

"Even Ethan told me that Jonathan is afraid of Mr. Griffin," I confessed.

"Really?" Willow asked.

"Yes."

"Well, you know kids, they don't like to snitch," Willow said, rolling her eyes.

"I think they've been threatened not to talk," I said softly.

"Sonya, I need you to do something I won't be able to do," Omar said.

"What's that?" I asked.

"I need you to steal all of Mr. Griffin's computer files with a flash drive," Omar answered.

"How the hell am I supposed to do that?" I asked.

"Why can't you do it? You're the police. Why the heck are you asking a citizen?" Willow asked.

"I'd have to get a warrant, and that's gonna take forever. If I go without one and I get caught, I'm done and kicked off the force," Omar said.

"I'll do it then, just give me what I need."

"I'm not sure if I approve of you breaking into another teacher's classroom. You were already on bad terms with him," Willow said.

"Trust me, Willow. We need to do this. You know in your heart that Mr. Griffin has been very suspicious for several years now," I urged.

"I don't know, Sonya. This sounds very dangerous," Willow replied.

"What if it was Beth? What would you do?" I asked.

Willow softly nodded and gave me her approval.

I had a small window of opportunity I needed to seize when Mr. Griffin went to lunch. He usually turned off his lights, but he left his door open. The hallway was quiet and empty. I quickly entered his classroom and softly shut the door behind me. I saw that he finished cleaning up the mess he had made.

I went over to his desktop computer and plugged in the flash drive Omar had given me. He told me that all I needed to do was plug it in and the drive would do the rest. It had a special software that would automatically clone the entire hard drive. That meant he could investigate all his files, photos, and documents on his own computer.

My heart was beating so loudly, my ears rang. I hoped and prayed that no one would walk in, especially Mr. Griffin. If he saw me, it was game over. I had no idea what I'd come up with. As I waited for the flash drive to finish copying everything, I explored his room and snooped through the drawers in his desk.

He had several pictures of himself and his baseball teams from every year he was head coach. The players seemed happy with him, but I doubt that told the whole story. Teenagers were experts at having and hiding secrets. I put everything back where it belonged to avoid future suspicion.

A black rectangular bag caught my eye at the bottom of his desk. It was hidden behind several plastic containers that were filled with paperwork and other teaching-related materials. In one of the containers was a small clear bottle with a dark brown liquid inside. I didn't have time to investigate it, so I ignored it.

I carefully slid out the bag and zipped it open. There was a laptop inside. I let my curiosity get the best of me and took it out. I placed it on the desk to check what he had inside. When I lifted it open, it had a passcode. I tried about 16 different combinations before I gave up. I was never going to guess that passcode. I noticed that the flash drive had finished downloading everything on the desktop. I safely removed it and plugged it into the laptop.

Omar told me it didn't matter if the computer had a passcode or not, it would still be able to clone everything. He told me that his *infotech* buddies in the police department had technology that could infiltrate the darkest corners of the internet. I believed him. The flash drive was able to start copying everything after a couple of minutes. However, it was going far slower. I grew anxious.

Lunch was over in 10 minutes and Mr. Griffin was due back any second. I placed the laptop on the floor beside the desk so that it would be hidden from the door. I got up and paced the room. I thought about what to do. I texted Omar that I needed him. He had requested to work on campus to follow up on leads.

The door swung open. It was too late.

"Oh, hey Sonya. Whatcha doing here?" Mr. Griffin asked.

"Hey, Mr. Griffin. I was uh— I needed to ask you something."

"Okay, what's that?" Mr. Griffin asked.

"I needed to ask you if it's okay that I came here to apologize."

I hoped that he didn't notice that I was fumbling over my words, desperately trying to come up with a plausible excuse as to why I was in his room in the dark when he wasn't there.

"Oh my gosh, of course. It's okay, Sonya. I appreciate that," Mr. Griffin said as he set his lunchbox down and walked towards me. I put my hands up and he stopped, his eyes flashing confusion.

"Sorry, I just wanted to make sure that you were paying attention."

"I know I'm an old goat, but I'm paying attention."

"I'm sorry I accused you of being sexually abusive towards minors. It was a very serious accusation, and I didn't have any evidence to back it up."

"Oh, well thank you so much, Sonya. That means a lot to me. I was just so perplexed when you came into my room and started hurling all these accusations at me, you know?" Mr. Griffin asked.

"Right, of course."

The laptop started making some subtle beeping noises which made me want to jump out of my skin. Mr. Griffin's eyes darted around the room as he searched for the source of the noise. I cleared my throat and tried to distract him.

"Do you forgive me? I am really sorry."

"Yes of course. I do forgive you, Sonya. It is okay. It's water under the bridge."

"Thank you, I appreciate that."

He awkwardly remained still as did I.

"Was that all?" Mr. Griffin chuckled.

"Yes."

I wanted to peek down to see if the cloning process was complete but that would've given me away. I had no idea how I was going to even get the flash drive and put his laptop back without him noticing. He was old but he wasn't blind. I was in quite the predicament. I needed Omar to show up.

I noticed that students were starting to hurry down the hallway to get to class. Lunch was officially over and if I didn't act fast, so was I.

"Well, we got our students coming back from class. I'm sure they'll be missing you by now. My kids are about to arrive as well," Mr. Griffin said.

"Oh I don't think they'll miss me. They'll be happy to get a substitute, so they don't get any work."

"You're not wrong about that. I'll walk you out, Sonya," Mr. Griffin said as he started towards the door.

I took the chance as his back was turned and squatted down to check the laptop. It still wasn't done. I couldn't believe my eyes. I was so shocked; I didn't notice Mr. Griffin glaring at me over my shoulder. I didn't even hear him creep up. I jumped, snatched his laptop off the ground and rushed towards the students' desks.

"Hey Sonya. What do you think you're doing?" Mr. Griffin asked.

"Nothing."

"You have a flash drive inserted in my personal laptop. Why is that?" Mr. Griffin asked.

"Oh that's nothing. You don't have to worry about it."

"Oh yeah? You're going through my things and you're telling me not to worry about it? That's rich, Sonya."

"I'm sorry, Mr. Griffin. I had to."

Mr. Griffin sighed and dryly laughed. He went to his door, brought down a blind that covered the window and locked it. My stomach churned as I took a few steps back before backing into a wall.

"Sonya, I need you to give me back the laptop," Mr. Griffin commanded as he slowly approached me.

"Don't come near me," I warned.

"I don't know what you think you're gonna find, but it's not what you're looking for," Mr. Griffin said.

"Why are you sweating then?"

"I'm not."

"Do not come near me, Mr. Griffin. It's over for you."

"You don't understand, Sonya. I'm not hurting anybody. It's nothing. No one is supposed to see it. It's just for me."

"Claude, what the *fuck* are you talking about?" I asked.

"It's just a couple of photos. It's for me. It's for no one else."

"You're scaring me."

"Have you not looked?"

"No."

"Oh. Well, then forget about what I was saying. I was just— I was just joking," Mr. Griffin chuckled.

He was shaking and bullets of sweat were trickling down his forehead.

"It's gonna be really hard to forget about that."

"Sonya, you're gonna ruin my entire life. I'm married. I have children and grandchildren. You will stain me forever. Do you want to be responsible for the destruction of an innocent man's life?" Mr. Griffin asked.

"You don't sound innocent to me."

As soon as I glanced down at the laptop's screen, Mr. Griffin reached into his pocket, took out a pocketknife and lunged at me. I yelped and used the laptop as a shield as he grabbed me and threw me to the ground. I tightly held onto the laptop as he pinned me down with his body and held the knife to my throat. My eyes stung with tears as he scowled at me with the angriest, blaze-filled eyes I had ever seen from him.

"Give me the laptop, Sonya. Give it to me now!"

"Please don't kill me. I'm a mother. I have two sons," I pleaded.

"I'm a father and I don't care. Let go of the laptop and give it to me," Mr. Griffin hissed.

I was trembling uncontrollably and had trouble breathing as the knife pushed farther and farther into my throat. I had to make a choice and I had to make it fast.

This man is about to kill me, I thought.

I did what I needed to do. I pushed the laptop into his chest, and he instantly grabbed it, dropping the knife onto my body. There was already students knocking on the door, wondering what all the commotion was about.

Mr. Griffin are you there?

What's all that noise?

Why does it sound like two people are wrestling?

Do you guys think he's doing the dirty?

He definitely has his pants off.

Mr. Griffin rolled off of me and sprinted towards the door. He quickly unlocked it, said hi to his students and fast-walked away. I put the knife in my pocket and got up. I didn't say anything to the students because I didn't want to frighten them, but they started to bombard me with questions.

Why was Mr. Griffin so sweaty?

Why are you sweaty?

What were you guys doing in here?

Why did he start running down the hall?

Isn't he married?

Before I could answer, Omar finally showed up.

"Hey Sonya, I got your text," Omar said.

"You couldn't have gotten here sooner?" I asked.

"Sorry, I was talking with my bosses. What happened?" Omar asked.

"Alright class, everyone sit down and wait for further instructions okay? Mr. Griffin will be back. Please behave yourselves. Thank you," I said.

I texted one of my colleagues to watch my class while I was gone. I lead Omar towards an empty computer lab to talk privately.

"What happened, Sonya? Why do you look flustered? What were you and Mr. Griffin doing?"

"Jesus, Omar. We were doing nothing. Like I would ever let that disgusting man put his hands on me like that."

"That's not what I meant."

"He attacked me."

"What? When?"

"He caught me cloning his laptop's hard drive and came at me with a knife."

"Where is he? Where did he go?"

"He ran down the hall with the laptop. I think he's still in the school."

Omar immediately notified the two officers on campus to find and detain Claude Griffin via his walkie talkie. He also had them inform Willow to issue a warning on him over the intercom. The school had to be placed under lockdown with all students, teachers, and faculty indoors.

"You're having the school go under lockdown?"

"...he is considered armed and dangerous...over," Omar radioed.

"I hope he doesn't hurt anyone else. I hope Santi's okay."

"They'll get him. This is nuts. He really attacked you?"

"I might have a mark on my neck."

Omar inspected me up close.

"You have a thin red line. Was he threatening to slit your throat? I'm about to go get this guy myself."

"No, wait. It's fine."

"*Attention, this is a code red. Attention this is a code red. All students, teachers and faculty members must remain indoors until I give the all clear. If you see Mr. Griffin, do not approach, and do not grant him entry into your classroom. I repeat, do not approach Mr. Griffin, and do not grant him entry into your classroom. He is considered armed and dangerous,*" Willow announced over the intercom.

"It's official. Mr. Griffin is a man on the run. Jesus Christ."

"I should've never let you do this. He could've killed you."

"It wouldn't have been that easy for him," I declared.

"Did you at least find what we were looking for?" Omar asked.

"After all that trouble, you're damn right I did," I said as I held up the flash drive.

I yanked it out the second Mr. Griffin took the laptop. I only hoped it still worked and that the download had been completed.

"Let's plug it in then."

We inserted it into a nearby computer and I let Omar access the police's computer program that allowed him to see all the files it had downloaded.

"There's a lot of corrupted data on here," Omar said.

"Don't tell me it didn't download. It was taking forever."

"You downloaded a decent amount of his files. Let's see what we got."

As Omar began opening files and pictures that he deemed suspicious, we were immediately horrified by the content. There was dozens of pictures of underage boys. None of them were wearing clothes. Some of them were performing disturbing sexual acts. It was extremely tough to get through. I found myself crying throughout it all. He also had several pictures of teenage boys changing in the boy's locker room. They had baseball uniforms on. He was an utter monster. It made me violently sick to my stomach.

"Omar, this is unbelievable," I choked out.

"I wanna kill this man. I want to end him," Omar angrily whispered.

Omar and I averted our eyes many times before we decided we had seen enough evidence that Mr. Griffin was most likely the most infamous sexual predator in the town of Skyview Falls. He also most likely had the largest child pornography collection in our town. It was absolutely horrific. It was pure evil that he had been allowed to be a teacher and a high school baseball coach for over 30 years.

Omar and I were beyond livid. That degenerate taught in the same school as me. He taught in the same school where my kids learned and where hundreds of other teenagers learned. He needed to be brought to justice immediately. Omar continued on and went through some of his files where he had dozens of accounts with different login details. The accounts belonged to illegal child pornography websites on the dark web. He seemed to have several secret memberships to many pedophilic forums, and photo-sharing sites.

"In all my years as a police officer, working on the street and in schools— I've never seen something like this. This is the devil's work."

"This whole time the rumors were real. Can you imagine what he did to the students who never spoke up?" I shuddered.

"Can you imagine what he did to Jonathan Locke?" Omar asked.

"You need to take him down, Omar," I urged.

"That motherfucker will never see the light of day for the rest of his life. I promise you," Omar proclaimed.

Get on the ground now!

Freeze or we will shoot!

We heard shouting outside the window of the lab and stood up to see what was going on. We ran to the window and saw two officers chasing Mr. Griffin in the courtyard. He was still clutching the laptop. Omar sprinted out of the lab without saying a word. I continued watching as the officers started gaining on him.

As Mr. Griffin approached the student parking lot, Omar came running out with his gun, bent down on one knee, aimed, and shot his gun twice in Mr. Griffin's direction.

I flinched as the gunshot sounds sliced through the air like thunderbolts, reverberating throughout the entire school. He collapsed to the ground, dropping the laptop, and grabbing his leg. He cried out and writhed in pain as Omar and the other officers charged at him to put him in handcuffs.

I sat down as my hands began to shake. The adrenaline coursing through my body seemed to dissipate as the reality of everything began to set in.

After all those years, Mr. Griffin did touch those boys. What would've happened if we never recovered his files and pictures? Would he have died an innocent man? I didn't like to think about it too much.

CHAPTER 12

Dozens of police officers and local news crews were on Skyview High's campus within the hour. It was breaking news across town and across the state. A widely loved, decorated history teacher and championship baseball coach, turned out to be a massive sexual predator and pedophile.

It trended on all social media platforms as millions of people were posting, and commenting on the horrors of the situation. It was already leaked that he had a giant collection of child pornography and that he had a hidden reputation of touching underage boys. Complete outrage was expressed at Skyview High's administration for allowing him to teach and coach for as long as he did. Willow was doing her best to navigate through the fallout.

I felt for her. It was a highly sensitive situation, and she simply didn't know he was a predator. Many people didn't. The scariest part about Mr. Griffin is how well he hid his true self from everyone.

A news reporter managed to record footage of Mr. Griffin being escorted into the police station while he was in handcuffs.

"Mr. Griffin! Is it true you inappropriately touched underage boys while coaching the baseball team?" The reporter asked.

"I'm sorry. I'm so sorry about it all. I shouldn't have touched those boys. I let my desires get the best of me. I'm so sorry to my wife and my children. Please don't hate me. I love you all so much! Please don't hate me! Please!" Mr. Griffin sobbed.

The video was cut short after that. I couldn't believe he had the nerve to feel remorse after everything he did. He wasn't sorry. He was sorry he got caught. I was in the courtyard giving Omar a statement.

"Here's the story, Sonya, if anybody asks. You saw him looking at the pictures of underage boys through his classroom window and he spotted you. That's when he attacked you and threatened you to keep quiet. You then called me, and I had probable cause to search through his computers," Omar said.

"That's not exactly what happened. You're okay not doing this by the book? I know how you are, and I respect how you work."

"These are special circumstances. The ends justify the means. Griffin is a monster from the deepest, darkest depths of hell. You did great work. No one needs to know the rest and no one's gonna ask too many questions anyway. Griffin is a roasted turkey," Omar said.

"I can live with that."

"I need a favor."

"What's up?"

"I need you to talk to Jonathan Locke. He's refusing to talk to us."

"You need to know about the murder weapon."

"We need to know what type of situation he was in. I don't want him to get charged with accessory to murder and evidence tampering.

He needs to know this is very, very serious. He was seen on video, hiding an alleged murder weapon."

"I'll talk to him. Did you pull him?"

"He's in Principal Jacobson's office," Omar said.

Willow and I sat across from Jonathan, who was very nervous. He was twitchy and had his head down as he anxiously tapped his foot.

"With everything that's happened, how are you feeling, Jonathan?" Willow asked.

"I don't know. I'm alright, I guess. Griffin just got shot and arrested for being a super rapey weirdo. Things feel really crazy to me right now. They're saying he's the biggest child rapist in the history of Skyview Falls. That guy taught history here since the second world war. Imagine that shit," Jonathan scoffed.

"We understand that completely. It is a very tragic and horrible situation," I said.

"So why am I here exactly? Am I in trouble again?" Jonathan asked.

"No, of course not. We just wanted to tell you that this is a safe space and that you can talk about anything," Willow kindly answered.

"You can tell us *anything*. We mean it. We won't judge you," I said.

"Did the police tell you to do this or something? I don't wanna talk to them again. I didn't do anything wrong," Jonathan pleaded.

"Look, Jonathan, the police are still very much aware of what you did in regard to the bloodied box cutter that you placed in Ethan's locker. They need to know why or there will be grave consequences," I said.

"Will I get arrested again?" Jonathan asked.

"You will be arrested again and there's a high chance they'll charge you with a crime," I said.

Jonathan buried his face in his hands and started sobbing.

"I don't wanna go to prison," Jonathan said through muffled cries.

"It's okay, Jonathan. You won't if you explain your side of the story," I said.

"Tell us what happened between you and Mr. Griffin," Willow added.

Jonathan raised his head and wiped his tears away. I offered him tissues. He sighed and gave each of us long, solemn stares.

"Do you really wanna hear this?" Jonathan asked.

"We do," I said.

"I wasn't doing that great in Mr. Griffin's class. I had a failing grade. We had a lot of late-night practices and when I got home I was too tired to do his homework or study for his tests. He gave us bi-weekly projects and I just couldn't keep up. They were worth so many grades. The bad grade I had in his class brought down my grade point average so low that I wasn't eligible to play basketball anymore. I was in danger of being kicked off the team. I couldn't let that happen. I love basketball more than anything. You have to understand that basketball is my ticket out of the bad life. I'm not good at school and

I'm not good at selling things. I'm good at basketball. It's the only thing my parents can be proud of about me. So I asked Mr. Griffin if there was anything I could do to raise my grades. That turned out to be the biggest mistake of my life," Jonathan explained.

"What happened?" I asked.

"He said I could do extra credit. What was the extra credit? It was me getting on my knees and giving him a…you know what. I really hated doing it, but I was desperate. He was rough too. He turned into someone else when we did that nasty shit. That was the tip of the iceberg," Jonathan said.

"Jesus Christ," Willow muttered.

"We're so sorry that happened, Jonathan. He took advantage of you. You have nothing to be ashamed of. He sexually abused you. You are the victim," I said.

Jonathan became teary-eyed.

"That went on for months. I was so ashamed. I didn't dare to talk about it to anyone. I felt like it was my fault. I was the one who accepted the offer. It was all my fault," Jonathan said.

"Someone like him shouldn't have been a teacher or a coach to begin with. It's not your fault," Willow offered.

"Frankly, he's a bastard, Jonathan. A degenerate bastard," I said strongly.

"Now, what happened with the box cutter?" Willow asked.

"I didn't know anything about it at the time. Griffin just forced me to put it inside Ethan's locker. He threatened to fail me if I didn't do it. He said if I got caught, there would be grave consequences. He scared the shit out of me. It had blood on it, and I really didn't want to do it, but Griffin threatened to make my life hell if I didn't do what he said," Jonathan confessed.

"This whole time. How did we know and not know at the same time? I'm gonna puke. This is obscene," Willow said.

"He was excellent at hiding who he really was," I said.

"He's the one who tipped off the police about the locker, anonymously," Jonathan said.

"That makes a lot of sense," I said.

"That's alarming," Willow said.

"Do you know how many other boys were abused?" I asked.

"I have an idea. I can give you names but I doubt they'll talk. We all had a silent agreement that we wouldn't talk about it. It probably wasn't the best idea," Jonathan muttered.

"It wasn't, but I get it. You boys shouldn't have been in that situation to begin with." Willow shook her head.

"Was Henry abused by him?" I asked.

Jonathan bent forward and clasped his hands together. He shook his head.

"He never said it out loud, no one ever did, but it was obvious. He would go into his office in the boy's locker room. They'd be alone for over an hour. There's no cameras in there. You can probably guess what went on in there," Jonathan said.

"My god," I gasped.

"You've gotta be kidding me. How long did this go on for?" Willow asked.

"A long time," Jonathan admitted.

"He deserves death," I demanded.

"I could tell Henry was getting sick of it towards the end. He was angrier and angrier as the days went on," Jonathan said.

"Do you think he started to refuse him?" I asked.

"I think so," Jonathan said.

"Maybe he threatened to expose him for everything," I said.

"And now he's dead," Jonathan said.

"You think Mr. Griffin murdered him because Henry threatened to expose all the horrible things he was doing?" Willow asked.

"It would make the most sense," I said.

"He had the murder weapon. It probably has Henry's blood on it. You guys do the math," Jonathan stated.

That was it. The case had been blown wide open. It had been Mr. Griffin all along.

"Okay, Jonathan. Thank you so much for telling us everything. You're gonna be a huge help to the police and you're gonna put Griffin behind bars for a very long time." Willow promised.

"I hope so," Jonathan grumbled.

"I have one more question. Did he ever touch my son?" I asked.

"I don't know, Ms. Salvador. You'd have to ask him that yourself," Jonathan said.

I joined Ethan on the couch as he watched basketball on the TV while doing his homework. I found it funny how he rapidly shifted his attention between the screen and the notebook in front of him.

"Are you sure you can do both things at the same time?" I asked.

"Don't worry, mom. I got this. I do a thing called multi-tasking."

"If you say so," I said.

"What the hell happened at school? I heard Mr. Griffin got shot and arrested. A whole bunch of crazy shit went down. It was all over Twitter. The guys told me that he had naked pictures of little boys on his computer. Is that true? That's disgusting as hell," Ethan said.

"Unfortunately, it is true. He's a truly revolting human being. He'll be locked away for a long time."

"Finally," Ethan said.

"You say that like you already knew something," I said.

"I heard that he touched boys on the baseball team. I didn't know about the kiddie porn. What a sicko."

"Ethan, I need to ask you an important question."

"What's up, mom?" Ethan asked.

"Did Mr. Griffin ever touch you inappropriately?"

Ethan placed his notebook aside and glanced at me.

"Yes. Yes, he did," Ethan admitted.

"Oh my god," I gasped as my heart skipped a beat. It ferociously pounded in my chest as I anxiously awaited what he was going to say next.

"I used to be on the junior varsity baseball team. This was in between basketball seasons."

"When on earth did you play baseball? I never knew this."

"I told you, but I guess you just assumed I was playing basketball. I know you used to mix up the sports a lot," Ethan said.

"I must've."

"He smacked my butt a lot in practice until I finally told him not to touch me. He tried telling me that it was common practice for a coach to smack a player's butt for doing well on the field," Ethan said.

"That's common practice? That's pedophilia!" I exclaimed.

"It is and it's weird, so I told him to stay away from me. When he did it again I almost shoved him to the floor. So he kicked me off the team. He never snitched on me though. I guess he knew how weird the story would sound if he did. *Oh yeah I kicked Ethan off the team because he didn't let me touch his butt.* It doesn't sound very appropriate."

"Ethan, you never told me about this. That is serious. I would've had that man thrown out of the school and would've demanded that they revoke his teaching license."

"I didn't think it was that big of a deal. I thought I handled it," Ethan shrugged.

He was just a teenager. He didn't know any better. For all he knew, it was an isolated incident. He didn't understand the ramifications of Mr. Griffin's actions. He didn't know what type of person he was. I couldn't blame him. I couldn't blame any of them. Mr. Griffin was the only one at fault. He was a monster. I brought Ethan in and hugged him.

"Mom, you're crushing me," Ethan squeaked out.

"Sweetheart, you need to tell me about these things. Okay? I need to know so I can help you."

"Am I in trouble?" Ethan asked.

"No, you're not in trouble."

"Do you think Mr. Griffin murdered Henry?" Ethan asked.

"I'm sure of it," I firmly stated.

Santi came barging in and jumped on top of us, joining in on the hug.

"Why are you guys group hugging without me?!" Santi asked.

We all warmly laughed. We needed that. It was the first true family moment we had after Ethan's release. All seemed well and things were looking up for Ethan. I should've known better.

CHAPTER 13

Chief Delatorre held a press conference in the town hall to speak on Mr. Griffin's various, horrific crimes. The county superintendent was there along with several other notable school district officials. Willow was there as well with the rest of Skyview High's administration. Omar stood beside the chief along with the other officers who apprehended Mr. Griffin. I allowed my class to watch the press conference from a digital projector.

It was one of the most infamous moments in the school's history. The insane part was, that it wasn't even the most infamous incident that year. That would be attributed to Henry's gruesome murder and subsequent mystery surrounding his case.

Chief Delatorre explained that Mr. Griffin would be charged with multiple counts of sexual misconduct, sexual assault, statutory rape as well as multiple counts of having possession of child pornography. He would go on to list other charges that would ensure that Mr. Griffin would not see the light of day for the rest of his life.

The school officials went on to speak and profusely apologized at the fact that Mr. Griffin had been employed for so long and that he had been allowed to be a high school baseball coach for many years. The truth was no one really knew until we found the deeply disturbing evidence on his computer. Jonathan speaking up and revealing what had happened behind closed doors all but confirmed it all. It wasn't just rumor. It was fact. The important thing was that he would never touch another boy again.

I found it odd that they did not mention Henry's murder in connection with Mr. Griffin. I thought they were going to announce that he was indeed the murderer or that he was a prime suspect in the ongoing investigation. I guessed that they were biding their time and trying to get out as much information as possible without riling up the public too much. If they found out that Mr. Griffin had sexually abused Henry and had murdered him, the entire town would've erupted. Lawrence and Veronica would've turned Skyview Falls upside down.

After the press conference, it didn't take long for Willow to call an emergency assembly in the auditorium to discuss recent events. The auditorium was packed to the brink of capacity and was so silent you could faintly hear the air conditioner humming. No one dared to speak as Willow was up on stage with a projector behind her. It had an image of Mr. Griffin in handcuffs.

"We thought we could trust Mr. Griffin. We thought we could put our faith in him. We thought he taught at this school because he genuinely cared about his students and wanted to see them succeed and learn about US history. It was all a lie, folks. I'm not sugarcoating anything. There were rumors of his behavior, but without evidence and testimony we couldn't do anything about it. That's the unfortunate part about all this. I wish I could've saved the many victims he abused. They may not be dead, but they've been scarred. They've been traumatized. It's hard to overcome that. He was a man that you trusted. He used that trust to bully you, to manipulate you and to use you for his own disturbing ends. I'm truly sorry this happened. He abused his power. He was a coward and a degenerate. I know it's hard to speak about the things he did, but the reality is…he would've been caught much sooner if his victims had spoken up earlier. I know it's selfish of me to ask, but think about this…how many lives could you save by speaking up? I urge you to do it for the future potential victims who might suffer under your code of silence. Again, I know it's selfish for me to ask, but this is the only way we can stop monsters like him. We have to speak up. We have to," Willow demanded.

The entire student body erupted into applause and cheered. If Willow knew how to do anything, it was public speaking. She thanked everyone for their applause and went on to discuss the importance of consent and spotting the early warning signs of sexual predators who are expert manipulators. Omar slipped in and motioned for me to come outside. I met him in the adjacent hallway that connected the building with the courtyard.

"I've got bad news," Omar sighed.

"What is it?" I asked.

"Griffin was in an AA meeting when the murder allegedly took place, and several witnesses confirmed it," Omar said.

"People he went to the meetings with?"

"Yeah and his wife confirmed it," Omar said.

"It's hard to believe he was ever a teacher," I hissed as I shook my head.

"He was also the championship baseball coach," Omar scoffed.

"You might as well throw him into the inferno now," I replied.

"I wish I had that power."

"What about the box cutter situation then?" I asked.

"We found Griffin's initials engraved on it so it's definitely his. He said someone stole it from his desk, used it to kill Henry then placed it back without anyone looking. He got nervous when he found it and forced Jonathan to hide it in Ethan's locker. This was around the time Henry was reported missing," Omar explained.

"Why Ethan's locker?"

"Most of the basketball guys know each other's combinations just in case one of them needs to borrow athletic clothing or a gym towel. Griffin picked Ethan because he saw the fight between him and Henry. He figured he would be a likely suspect in Henry's disappearance. He also feared that Henry had been murdered with his own knife," Omar revealed.

"He is the slimiest bastard I've ever seen, and I was married to Felix for 10 years," I said.

"I was so ready to get him on Henry's murder, Sonya. I thought we finally had our guy."

"The security cameras didn't show you who took the box cutter from the classroom?" I asked.

"Nope, I checked. Whoever did it was smart enough to do it when class either began or ended. We don't see anyone going in alone except for Mr. Griffin. All we saw was Jonathan coming out and planting it in Ethan's locker."

"If Mr. Griffin didn't kill Henry then who the hell did?"

"The lab results finally came back for the box cutter. I don't even know if I should be telling you all this."

"I'm not gonna tell anyone anything. I also think I deserve it after almost getting my throat slit by that scumbag."

"You can't say this to anyone."

"Why are you acting weird?" I asked.

"Look, Henry's blood was on the box cutter, so it's now confirmed to be the murder weapon. Jonathan's blood was also on it, but we know he cut himself with the knife while he was planting it."

"Okay, that was a given," I said.

Omar came closer and looked around.

"Omar, what is it?" I asked.

"The reason it took so long was because there was another person's blood on it," Omar whispered.

"Who?"

"Felix," Omar breathed.

Felix's blood.

"What? What are you saying?" I asked.

"Felix's blood is on the murder weapon."

"Does he know? Is there a reason why?"

"Apparently he mishandled it in the evidence locker and cut himself. It's sharp. He never even bothered to tell anyone. Chief Delatorre and the lead detectives on the case are very pissed. I wouldn't be surprised if they suspended him. He wasn't supposed to be touching it," Omar shook his head.

"Jesus, Omar. What the hell is Felix doing?"

"I have no idea."

"Do you really believe he mishandled it? How do you mishandle a knife?"

"I don't know. It's very sketchy, but they wouldn't dare arrest him. They'll chalk it up to severe negligence on his part."

"It wouldn't be the first time."

"He'll wiggle out of it. They like him enough. He's smooth, but that's about it," Omar admitted.

"I fell for it once. I won't make that mistake again."

"Don't blame yourself. It was all him. I saw it with my own eyes. He buried himself with his own inner demons," Omar offered.

"It was probably all the lies he told me. After a while I didn't know what truth even meant to him or if it even existed to him," I sighed.

Omar tenderly put his hand on my shoulder and squeezed.

"I'm sorry this case hasn't been resolved yet. Just when I think I'm untangling the threads of Henry's murder mystery, they tangle up again into tighter knots," Omar scoffed.

"You and me, both."

As I drove home that night, I couldn't stop thinking about the DNA results from the box cutter. Felix's blood had been on the murder weapon. That was a cold, hard fact. I felt his explanation as to why it was on there was very shaky. I decided to find him. I dropped off Santi at home and sped over to where he always was whenever he didn't have the kids and was off work.

It was called *The Pourhouse*. It was a popular, rustic place that was lively and boisterous during evening hours. The atmosphere was typically charged with drunken energy and excitement, especially when there was a big sporting event playing on the flat screen TVs. The dimly lit space was furnished with neon signs, vintage rock 'n' roll posters, sports memorabilia and a snazzy jukebox inserted into a corner near their billiards lounge. The air was thick with animated conversations, roaring laughter, and the occasional cheering.

I spotted Felix sitting at the bar, drinking, and laughing away with Stanley, his cop buddy. I shoved my way through the rowdy crowd and avoided the giant, muscled men with black leather jackets and satanic tattoos for obvious reasons. I sat next to Felix with his back turned and requested a water from the bartender. I tapped him on the shoulder. When he turned around and saw me, a glowing smile spread across his face.

He's drunk, I thought.

"Hey baby, I knew you couldn't stay away," Felix slurred.

He's definitely drunk.

"Sorry ma'am, he's had a lot to drink," Stanley commented.

"Stanley! What the hell man! You're ratting me out!" Felix shouted.

"Felix, keep your voice down," I commanded.

"Sonya, you remember Stanley? He's the asshole who wouldn't let us see Ethan when he got arrested," Felix laughed.

"Thanks Felix," Stanley replied.

"Oh, I'm kidding you snot-nosed prick. He's a tight-ass, Sonya. Don't worry about him," Felix shrugged.

"Can we talk outside?" I asked.

"You wanna talk with me?" Felix asked.

"Yes, outside. It's too loud in here," I said.

"Whatever, that's cool. I'll be back, Stan man," Felix said as he followed me outside.

I made sure to take my glass of water with me.

"Alright, we're outdoors. What do you want? You want to suck on my johnson or what?" Felix asked.

I splashed the water in his face. He flinched back and sputtered.

"Sonya! What the hell?!"

"Are you sobered up now? I need to talk to you about something serious," I scolded.

"You just assaulted a police officer. I can have you arrested," Felix said.

"It was water, you whiny baby. You're not arresting anyone, Felix. Listen to me carefully," I said.

"What the hell do you want? Just spit it out already," Felix snapped as he dried his face with his shirt.

"Where were you the night Henry was murdered?" I asked.

"What? Why are you asking me that?" Felix asked.

"Answer the question," I commanded.

"I don't know, I was probably out getting my drink on, or I was working a night shift. I don't remember. I didn't even see the kid that day," Felix said.

"Why was your blood on the box cutter? The murder weapon in Henry's case."

"I mishandled evidence, sweetheart. It happens."

"Why were you even handling it?" I asked.

"I was down there for something else, and I wanted to check it out while I was there. I think knives are interesting objects," Felix said.

"I don't buy that. You mishandled it while you were slashing Henry's throat, didn't you?" I asked.

Felix was taken aback and threw his hands up in the air.

"Now hold on a second. What the hell are you getting at?" Felix asked.

"You heard me."

"Why in god's name would I ever do that?" Felix asked.

"I don't know. Why would you?" I asked.

"I loved Henry, okay? I loved him like a son. I would never, *ever*, kill him."

"I almost believe you."

"Why wouldn't you believe me?" Felix asked.

"You had a lot of secrets during our marriage, Felix. You're a good liar,"

"Secrets, secrets, secrets, Sonya. That's all you ever talk about," Felix hissed.

"That's all you ever have," I snapped.

"Fine! It's true. I have secrets and I lie a lot, but I've changed. I swear to you that I have. I don't lie anymore, and I don't have any more secrets," Felix stated.

"How do I know you're not lying again?" I asked.

"I guess you don't," Felix said as he turned heel and stumbled back into the bar.

Why would Felix murder Henry? I thought as I walked back to my car. I stayed parked and cleared my head. There really wasn't a logical reason why he would murder him. Felix was fond of Henry. He would cheer him on at almost all of his basketball games. He cheered for Henry more than Ethan at times. What if Henry knew something he shouldn't have? What could he have had on Felix? It would have to have been something big. Something that would destroy his entire life. The same question continued to echo in my mind as I drove home.

Why would Felix murder Henry?

CHAPTER 14

I was eating in the cafeteria with the English teachers when it happened. As usual, they were chirping and gossiping away while I minded my business. I kept an eye on Layla. She was sitting alone at a faraway corner table. She slowly ate her mashed potatoes and green peas while she stared into space. I felt bad for her. She usually ate with Ethan.

It was nice to have company in high school. I knew how hard and miserable it was to be a loner. Because of how I was raised, I kept people at arm's length for a long time. That only changed after a long period of self-reflection.

In a lot of ways, Felix helped me break out of my shell. He showed me how to let my guard down and then betrayed me, making me question my worth and who I was as a person. I wished he had stayed the best version of himself. He was a good one in the beginning. I still remember our first conversation. It was in college, and I was studying outside in a grassy field, near the campus' central square.

16 YEARS AGO

The college I went to had a sprawling landscape marked with lush green lawns, towering trees, and massive buildings that housed marble columns and shiny linoleum floors. The campus buzzed with a constant flow of students rushing to and from classes, carrying backpacks filled with laptops, notebooks, and textbooks. It was my first time away from home and I loved how the air was filled with a tangible sense of excitement and new opportunities. That's what I needed. A fresh start. When a dashing, handsome young man with chiseled arms and a well-groomed beard approached me in uniform, I thought I was about to have it all. I thought my life was destined to change for the better. How wrong I was.

We all lie to save ourselves.

"Hey there little lady," a deep voice rang out.

Startled, I glanced up and saw him for the first time. It was Felix Salvador when he was twenty-four years old. My heart fluttered. I had no idea why he would want to talk to me. I was alone and not that social. I didn't look very approachable. I wore a long floral dress that covered up most of my body. My hair was in a ponytail, and I had white sneakers on. People said I had a weird sense of style back then. In the end I really didn't know why he was drawn to me.

"Hi. Am I in trouble, officer?" I asked.

"Oh god, no. Sorry, I forget the police uniform scares some people," Felix said as he sat down beside me.

"It's okay," I grinned.

"What's your name?" Felix asked.

"I'm Sonya."

"It's very nice to meet you. I'm Felix."

"It's nice to meet a police officer," I replied.

"So, I was bored, and you looked like you could use some company," Felix said.

"I'm studying but it's fine."

"Sorry, I don't want to interrupt you. You sure it's okay?" Felix asked.

"Yeah, it's okay."

"Good, good. I'm supposed to be patrolling campus, but nothing ever happens around here. My partner can handle it if anything."

"How long have you been a cop?" I asked.

"Oh, about three years. My dad was a cop and his dad too so naturally I enlisted in the family trade. We're simple men who like the simple things in life."

"That makes sense."

"What about you, little lady? What are you studying?" Felix asked.

"Education, I'm gonna be a teacher."

"Oh wow, okay. That's really nice. You'll be educating the youth. That's very important. I respect that job. It's not easy."

"I respect your profession as well. Being a police officer can't be easy. I imagine it comes with many risks."

"It does, Sonya, but I love it. I love it more than gravy. I wouldn't wanna do anything else," Felix said.

"What do you love the most about being a cop?" I asked.

"I love helping people out. I love how I have the power to do that. You know what I mean?" Felix asked.

"I understand that."

"I can tell you're gonna be a great teacher."

"How's that?"

"You're a very nice lady."

"I'm a lady? I'm pretty sure you're older than me."

"I'm twenty-four. What about you?"

"I'm nineteen."

"Wow, I thought you were older. You speak like a grown woman."

"I get that a lot, people say I'm mature for my age," I said proudly.

"They're right, you sound wise."

"I had to grow up fast in my family."

"How come?"

"I'd rather not talk about it, I went through a lot. Let's just say I had a bad childhood," I said.

"Hey, that's okay. We don't have to talk about it."

"Sorry."

"No, it's okay. Tell you what though, I have an exam coming up and I could use some help studying for it. Would you be able to help me?" Felix asked.

"What exam?" I asked.

"The exam is about winning over Sonya's heart. I really need to ace it," Felix smiled.

I laughed as he winked at me. He was a warm, funny guy once. *Once.* Felix's charm infected everyone he spoke with. It was easy to love the guy.

"That was really corny," I grinned.

"It did make you laugh though."

"Alright, fine. I'll help you study."

"You like beer?" Felix asked.

"I don't drink, and I can't drink. I'm underage."

"Holy shit, that's right. That's fine. We won't drink."

"We can do other things instead," I replied cheekily.

I didn't know where that had come from, but he brought it out of me.

"Damn girl. I can tell you and I are gonna get along just fine," Felix said.

The rest was history. We clicked right away and began dating. I got pregnant not long after that and we got married. Every now and then I thought back to those first couple of years with Felix. It was near bliss. After that it was filled with secrets, lies, arguments, drunken rants, broken plates, and a love that turned to stone.

PRESENT DAY

As I snapped back to reality, I saw two students approach Layla. One was Jeff Toledo and the other was Wyatt Rojas. They had a reputation for being strange boys. Ethan told me they smoked a lot of pot. Layla awkwardly looked up at them as they took out their phones and showed her a picture I couldn't see. They were telling her something, but I couldn't hear a thing. She looked upset and waved them off. She wanted them to go away. Jeff climbed on top of a nearby lunch table and held up his phone. I instinctively stood up.

"Layla Forrester killed Henry! It's on Reddit and Twitter! Read the theories! They make sense! Justice for Henry! We want justice for Henry!" Jeff shouted.

Layla and I locked eyes from across the cafeteria. We were both mortified. I think it was safe to say that Jeff had lost his marbles. Three security guards rushed towards Jeff to get him down. He surrendered and was promptly taken to the principal's office for disorderly conduct. Layla was shaking as the entire cafeteria stared at her. The English teachers chirping away didn't help matters.

Why would Jeff say something like that?

Do you think it's true?

Layla does look suspicious.

Her boyfriend is the killer after all.

I couldn't take it anymore. I banged my hand on the table and shut them up.

"Don't you ladies have anything better to do than to gossip all day? Jesus. It is exhausting listening to all your nonsense," I snapped.

They all gaped at me and remained silent. When Layla ran out of the cafeteria with watery eyes, I quickly followed her out. She was outside in the courtyard, sitting behind a vending machine. I sat down next to her.

"Hey Layla," I said.

"Hey Ms. Salvador."

"Are you okay?"

"I'll be fine," Layla said as she wiped her tears on her sleeve.

"I'm sorry about what Jeff said. He's an idiot. Don't listen to him."

"You know why he's saying that stuff right?" Layla asked.

"No, why?"

"After they said on the news that they weren't prosecuting Mr. Griffin for Henry's murder, these other murder theories started getting popular on Reddit and Twitter," Layla explained.

"What theories?"

"They're saying I killed him. They're saying it's a known fact that Henry was inappropriately touching girls and that I wanted revenge because he— I don't even wanna say it."

"What did they say about you, Layla?"

"They said he felt up my private parts. I don't want to go into detail. It was gross."

"The internet is horrible. What else is new?"

"When is Ethan coming back? I miss him."

"He told me he needed a couple of weeks. He misses you too. You're always welcome to come by."

"Thank you. You've always been nice to me."

I put my arm around her and pulled her in.

"You've made my son very happy. I can't complain. You're his one bright spot in this whole mess."

"I need to tell you something."

"What is it?" I asked.

"Ethan knew."

"He knew what?"

"He knew that Henry touched me in places he shouldn't have. I told him it wasn't just him messing around. He already knew about that. I told him he violated me."

"Oh my god, Layla. How far did this go?"

"He touched me at two separate parties. We were alone and he took advantage. I didn't tell Ethan right away because I knew they were best friends. I was confused and sad. Henry was always nice to me. I don't know why he would do that to me. Why would he do that, Ms. Salvador? He knew I was Ethan's girlfriend, his best friend's girlfriend. Why would he hold me down and stick his fingers inside me?" Layla cried.

My stomach dropped as I held Layla closer. I was horrified at what Henry had done to her and I was so angry for her. She didn't deserve any of it.

"It wasn't your fault, Layla. It was his. He should've never laid his hands on you. He was very wrong for that. He was no better than Mr. Griffin."

"I just wished he had never done that. I wished things were normal."

"What did Ethan do when you told him?" I asked.

"He had a huge argument with him. I think that's the reason why they fought."

Oh shit, I thought.

"That would make a lot of sense."

"Ms. Salvador, he told me that he wanted to kill him."

Oh no.

"He would never go through with it. He's not that type of person."

Right?

"I know, he just really scared me when he told me that."

"Ethan is not a murderer."

He can't be.

"There's another theory floating around that I killed Henry, and that Ethan helped me dump the body since I wouldn't have been able to carry it myself."

"That's insanity. You guys aren't murderers."

"Tell that to that idiot, Jeff."

"Don't worry about him, he's in big trouble."

"Why is this happening to me and Ethan? What did we do to deserve this?" Layla asked.

"How did these theories even start?" I asked.

"Someone posted a picture from Jonathan Locke's Instagram. Henry and I were in the background. It was taken after school on the day he was murdered."

"How can they possibly know it was taken that day?" I asked.

"Jonathan captioned the date in roman numerals. He does that for all his posts. It's a trend I guess."

"Go figure."

I took Ethan and Layla to *Moe's Diner*. A seldom-known, retro establishment in Skyview Falls that was a hidden gem. I knew the intoxicating aroma of sizzling burgers, freshly brewed coffee, creamy milkshakes, and homemade chocolate chip cookies would help them forget about the exhaustive ordeal they were going through. I needed the distraction as well. The interior was decorated with vintage memorabilia that included black and white photographs as well as chrome accent tables, bright red booths, and a checkered floor. The diner had a sense of escapism that I needed when I was younger. I would escape the chaos of my household often by going there.

We sat down and looked at the menu. The diner was mostly empty. I had been counting on that. All eyes seemed to be on my poor son and his girlfriend. I wished I had the ability to blow them all to hell so that they could live their lives in peace and finish high school with clear minds. It was hard to concentrate on an Algebra test when murder accusations echoed in the back of your head.

We ordered and they heartily devoured all their food when it came. It was my favorite sight to see as a mom.

"You wanna know why I was even near him that day?" Layla asked.

"Why?" I asked.

"I was gonna tell Principal Jacobson what he had been doing to me and Beth. She's a girl I met in study hall. I found out that he had been touching her too," Layla said.

"I know Beth. She's so sweet. I can't believe Henry did that shit, man," Ethan said.

"Do you still talk to Beth?" I asked.

"Yeah, of course. She just doesn't have the same lunch as me. We're in different grades. She's Principal Jacobson's daughter. She didn't tell me that, I found out later," Layla explained.

"She probably likes to keep that under the radar," Ethan replied.

"I've been meaning to ask you something, Layla. I know we came here to not talk about what everyone else has been talking about but—," I trailed.

"It's okay, it's inevitable. We had a good laugh for a while, but this whole thing isn't over yet," Layla said.

"It should be. It's ridiculous. They need to leave us alone already," Ethan said.

"I saw you at the search party. The one for Henry. You saw me but you ran off. You looked shocked."

I almost said guilty, but I wanted to believe that Layla had nothing to do with it. I felt rude for even bringing it up, but I needed to know. That thought had been plucking at the corner of my mind for days. Deep down, I needed to protect Ethan. Everything I did was for him. I kept reminding myself that through it all. I wasn't able to be at peace until Henry's case was closed and the mystery behind his murder was solved. Only then would Ethan be able to live a normal life again.

"Wait, you went to that?" Ethan asked.

"Well, yeah. I genuinely wanted to help. But then everyone started saying he was dead, and I freaked out. When Veronica Cain started screaming I knew that things were *bad* and that I needed to get out of there," Layla said.

"Yeah, it was a horror show," I admitted.

Ethan put his arm around her and kissed her on the cheek.

"I'm gonna kill those Reddit virgins for messing with my girl," Ethan said.

"Do you think it's smart to say things like that out loud?" I asked.

"There's literally no one around," Ethan said.

"Still, Ethan. You should be careful. The walls have ears," I said.

"Your mom has a point, baby," Layla said.

"You've only been accused of murder," I said.

"I get it, mom. I've only heard that thousand times," Ethan said.

The bell at the front door rang. When I looked up I saw Jonathan walking in with three friends. They all wore athletic warm-ups and were on the basketball team.

"That's funny," I mumbled.

"What's up, mom?" Ethan asked.

He turned around and saw his teammates. They waved to him, he reluctantly waved back.

"What are they doing here?" Ethan asked.

"I guess I'm not the only one who knows about this place," I said.

"Why would they be here at the same time as us. Did they follow us?" Ethan asked.

"I'm sure it's a coincidence," Layla said.

"Yeah, honey," I said.

"Nah, I don't trust him," Ethan said.

"Who, Jonathan?" I asked.

"Yeah. He put that box cutter in my locker. He can burn in hell," Ethan said.

"Ethan don't say that. You don't know the full details of that situation," I said.

"What are the full details then?" Ethan asked.

"I can't tell you that," I said.

"Why?" Ethan asked.

"Ethan, it's police business."

"How do you know then?" Ethan asked.

"It has to do with the school, and I helped with an investigation."

"Yeah, sure," Ethan grumbled.

"I'm telling the truth," I urged.

"Omar probably told you everything," Ethan said.

"He was my handler, yes," I said.

"Yeah, I bet," Ethan replied.

"Are you trying to suggest something?" I asked.

"Baby, why are you acting like this?" Layla asked him.

"You know people have whispered about it. They whisper about it in the halls, bathrooms, and locker rooms. They say Omar is smashing Ms. Salvador. You don't get how pissed off I get when I hear that filth," Ethan snapped.

Ethan was behaving very erratically, and I was beginning to seriously worry about him. I knew the murder case had him on edge, but he was crossing a line.

"I'm very sorry you have to hear that. I can assure you that Omar and I do not have any sort of romantic relationship. Okay?" I asked.

"Yeah, whatever," Ethan said.

"Baby, don't be like that," Layla said.

"I need to talk to Jonathan," Ethan declared as he got up and stomped towards him before we could react. We both watched on in anticipation as we quietly told him to come back.

"Layla, be honest. Is he on drugs?" I asked.

"I wish he was. It would explain his weird behavior," Layla shook her head.

All we could do was wait and see. It was like watching an impending car crash unfold in real time. You knew it was coming and there was nothing you could do to stop it.

"What's up Ethan?" Jonathan asked.

"Why do you have that picture up on your Instagram?" Ethan asked.

"What picture?" Jonathan asked.

"The one where Henry and Layla are in the background," Ethan said.

"I don't know. I didn't even notice them," Jonathan said.

"Bullshit. How didn't you see them?" Ethan asked.

"Dude, are you okay?" Jonathan asked.

"No, I'm not okay. I'm not in police custody anymore but I still have people online calling me a murderer and now they're calling my girlfriend one too. If you didn't have that stupid picture up, none of this would've happened," Ethan said.

"Sorry, dude. I don't know what to tell you," Jonathan said.

"I have a problem with you," Ethan threatened.

"Oh my lord," I muttered.

"Ethan come back here," Layla demanded.

"Honey, stop this right now," I said.

Ethan held up his hand, indicating that he wasn't gonna stop.

"Ethan, I'm gonna get up and get over there if you don't come back here this instant," I said.

"You should listen to your mommy," Jonathan mocked.

"You put the box cutter in my locker. Why?" Ethan asked.

"I'm not going to tell you anything," Jonathan shot back.

"You tried to frame me. I went to jail because of you!" Ethan shouted.

"Dude, it wasn't like that!" Jonathan exclaimed.

"Everyone thinks I murdered my best friend because of you!" Ethan's voice cracked as he lunged at Jonathan and pulled him out of the booth.

Layla and I were already on our feet. He landed a couple of blows to Jonathan's jaw as Jonathan tried to claw his face. Jonathan's friends shoved Ethan to the floor and started kicking him. I stepped in and screamed at them to stop.

Layla helped Ethan up and we jointly held him back as he struggled to break free. He wanted to continue. The son I raised wanted to continue a fist fight. We were forced to drag Ethan away as Jonathan's friends held him back.

"You're crazy, Ethan! You're a lunatic! You don't know the whole story!" Jonathan shouted.

"I don't need to!" Ethan said.

"Maybe the theories are right! Maybe you and Layla did kill him. Everyone knew Henry liked to mess around. He wasn't a sexual predator like Griffin for Christ's sake. It wasn't his fault your bat-shit crazy girlfriend couldn't take a joke! You didn't have to kill him for it!" Jonathan yelled.

"You don't know the whole story either or you wouldn't be saying that you stupid son of a bitch!" Ethan roared.

"You had a reason, Ethan. Everyone knows you did it. *Everyone*!" Jonathan bellowed.

Ethan stayed quiet as we left the diner. I gave my sincerest apologies to the staff for having to witness that very upsetting situation. It was crickets in the car on the ride back home for the longest time. I decided to break the silence.

"I cannot believe you did that, Ethan. I cannot believe I just saw that happen," I said.

"Oh, here we go," Ethan groaned.

"Here we go, nothing. I am very disappointed. That was very unnecessary and barbaric. You fought with him over a stupid picture. Are you serious?" I asked.

"It was his fault," Ethan whined.

"It's no one's fault, Ethan. If you wanna blame anyone, blame those idiots on the internet for coming up with those stupid theories," I said.

"I don't even know who they are. Their profile pictures are frog memes and old politicians with cowboy hats," Ethan said.

"You should've just ignored it then. I know it's tough and I know it's a very unfortunate situation but guess what? You're not making it any better by fighting yet another teammate in public," I scolded.

"It's not like he's gonna go missing," Ethan said.

"That was pretty scary, and you promised you wouldn't get into another fight," Layla said.

"I know, I know. I'm sorry," Ethan apologized.

"You'll be lucky if no one recorded it," Layla said.

Ethan heavily sighed.

"Oh, wouldn't that be spectacular?" I asked.

"In my defense, he put that stupid box cutter in my locker. He was trying to frame me!" Ethan bellowed.

"It's a lot more complicated than that," I said.

"How is it complicated?!" Ethan asked.

"He was sexually abused by Mr. Griffin, Ethan. He was forced to put the box cutter in your locker. Okay?"

"Wait, what? Mr. Griffin forced him? How?" Ethan asked.

"I can't give you the specifics. I just need you to trust me on this," I said.

"Oh my god," Layla whispered.

"How badly did he abuse him?" Ethan asked softly.

"It's even worse than what you're thinking," I said.

"Oh shit," Ethan cursed.

"Exactly," I uttered.

"I didn't know that he was forced to do that," Ethan said innocently.

"Now you do," I said.

"Mr. Griffin really might be the most depraved sexual predator in our town's history," Layla said.

"Not *might*, Layla. He is," I firmly stated.

"Why didn't we ever say anything?" Ethan whispered aloud.

He rested his head on Layla's shoulder and she held him. I didn't know what to think after my son's fight with Jonathan. Ethan's anger and aggression was foreign to me. Everything I knew about him felt like a lie. I felt like I had my own perfect image of who he should've been and didn't pay attention to who he *actually* was.

I didn't know if I was going crazy, but I saw a darkness in Ethan's eyes when he was fighting Jonathan in that diner. A darkness I had only seen twice in my entire life. In my father and in my ex-husband.

CHAPTER 15
BEFORE

We sat in a jam-packed basketball gym. There was a deafening roar from the crowd that shook walls and nearly brought the ceiling down. I was exaggerating of course, but it was *loud*. That was your typical basketball home game. A monumental event for a small town like ours. I was with Felix, Veronica, Lawrence, and Santi. We all cheered Ethan and Henry on as they took on their state rivals. That game was years ago, before I divorced Felix. The boys were younger, and playing in a traveling basketball league, competing with other amateur teams. They played on a team called the Sentinels while they faced the opposing team, the Shockers.

The atmosphere was electric and filled with so much intensity and anticipation, you could feel it seeping into your veins. The sports crowds at Skyview High were always infectious, where the game was being played. It was like stepping into a rock concert with over 30,000 raving fans. Ethan and Henry did their signature handshake as the game was set to begin.

"How much do you think the superstar is scoring tonight, Lawrence?" Felix asked.

"I'm not quite sure," Lawrence said.

"Thank you for nothing, Lawrence," Felix joked.

Lawrence remained stone-faced as Felix laughed at him.

"How much do you think Ethan will score?" Santi said.

"I'm not sure. This might not be his game. The Shockers have a lot of big bodies. Ethan's gonna have trouble driving to the basket," Felix said.

"Ethan's tough. He can do it!" Santi said.

"I guess," Felix muttered.

"You don't have faith in our son?" I asked.

"No, of course. Of course I do," Felix promised.

"I know my Henry is going to have a spectacular game. I'm gonna get it all on video and put it on Facebook. All my fans from *Veronica's Vices* are gonna tune in. Maybe I should go live. I should go live right?" Veronica asked.

"Maybe this isn't the best time," Lawrence said.

"Don't be a sourpuss," Veronica teased.

"I think it's a good idea. I'll help you set it up," Santi said.

"Oh I know how to do it sweetie. I'm old but not that old!" Veronica shrieked with laughter.

"She's a little crazy, don't mind her," I whispered to Santi

"I noticed."

We both giggled.

"What are you guys laughing at?" Veronica asked.

"I told her you're a little crazy," I replied.

"Bitch, so are you!" Veronica said.

We all jointly laughed up a storm, the boys looked at us like we were crazy.

"Guys, the game is starting. They're going to the center of the court," Santi mentioned.

"Rebounding! Defense! Dive for loose balls! Drive the baseline! Pump fakes! Draw fouls!" Felix shouted.

"Do you have to do this every game?" I chuckled.

"They need a gentle reminder," Felix said.

"You call shouting, gentle?" I asked.

"To me it's gentle," Felix said.

"Whatever you say," I said.

Felix grabbed my face and planted a loud, affectionate kiss on my lips.

"It is whatever I say, honey," Felix said.

The Sentinels won the tip, and the game was underway. Both teams sprinted up, and down the court with tremendous speed and agility. They ran so hard their sneakers squeaked hard against the polished surface of the basketball court. Every single time each team had the ball they tried their best to make it count. Every possession mattered in a game like that.

Whenever our team would shoot the ball, the crowd would hold their collective breath. It would majestically soar through the air, and if it swished through the net, the crowd erupted with thunderous applause. When Ethan and Henry scored points for our team, we jumped out of our seats and chanted their names. Except Lawrence. He was allergic to excitement.

As the game neared it's exhilarating end, the players pushed their physical limits by diving for loose balls, and catapulting into the air for every crucial rebound. They did everything in their power to try and achieve victory. Ethan and Henry led the offensive charge as the final minutes dwindled down. All of our hearts were racing as the final buzzer sounded. We had won. The crowd became a booming wall of cheering and applause as players from both teams shook hands with one another. We all rushed down, and waited outside for the boys as they celebrated amongst themselves.

When they came out, we all clapped for them.

"Holy shit! What a game!" Felix cheered.

"Dude you guys were so clutch!" Santi added.

"I know right?" Henry asked.

"We played hard, Santi," Ethan said, panting.

"That was so exciting. Your father is very proud of you, Henry," Veronica said.

"The old man looks like he's about to fall asleep," Henry said as he gave Lawrence a hug.

"Good game, son," Lawrence said.

When they let go, Felix unexpectedly hugged Henry. Ethan was left in the dust as he had gone to approach his father. I hugged him instead.

"You're insane, kid! You had 36 points and 13 rebounds! Video game numbers!" Felix shouted.

"You played incredible, Ethan," I said.

"Thanks mom," Ethan muttered as he let go.

He was obviously annoyed at Felix who was giving all his love to Henry.

"Ethan had a great game too, dad! He had 18 points and 4 three-pointers!" Santi said.

"What? Oh, yeah. I know. I know," Felix said as he let go of Henry.

"Both boys are superstars. There's a reason they're best friends," Veronica said.

"Yeah, for sure. I just had to give my love to Henry here. He was a beast. I mean, my god. You rarely ever see a stat line like that in a high school basketball game," Felix said.

"We get it, dad," Ethan snapped.

"Oh c'mon son, don't be like that. You played well too." Felix winked.

"Hey man, I love you. You're my brother. We're brothers for life, remember that," Henry voiced.

Ethan strongly nodded, and pointed back.

Brothers for life.

That's how serious sports was, for Ethan and Henry. That's how passionate they were for basketball. It revolved around their entire friendship. They went through many victories, losses, heartbreaks, and triumphs together. It was their ultimate purpose to succeed on that basketball court.

PRESENT DAY

I decided to grade papers during my lunch period. I also planned to eat inside my own classroom. I couldn't exactly sit with the other English teachers after I had yelled at them. Ethan and Layla walked in, giving me a welcome surprise. I was still irked with Ethan after his fight with Jonathan, but I decided to let that go for the time being. Life wasn't treating him well at the moment and things were already getting more difficult. I hated seeing him suffer. It gave me as much pain as it gave him.

We all lie to save ourselves.

The thought echoed in my mind. Did that mean I was lying to myself when it came to my son?

"Oh, hey. You're here," I said.

"I had to give some homework to Warren. He doesn't understand the whole online thing. It gives him a rash apparently. Dad dropped me off," Ethan said.

"We also had other things to handle. Tell her, Ethan," Layla added.

"That's not important right now. You tell her about the thing," Ethan urged.

"No, you go first," Layla shot back.

"Baby, it's not that important," Ethan snapped.

"What's going on?" I asked.

"I quit the team," Ethan blurted out.

"You did what?" I asked.

"I don't wanna play with those guys anymore. I saw the way they looked at me, like I was a killer."

"I thought they were your friends," I said.

"You really think they're still my friends after my fight with Jonathan? Truth is, they turned on me the second I was arrested. Screw them!" Ethan exclaimed.

"I can't believe this. I thought you all treated each other like brothers," I said, confusion washed over my face.

"They always liked Henry more anyway. I'm not interested in popularity contests. I'll transfer to another school next year with another team. I'll take the bus if I have to."

"Are you sure this is what you want? You have so much history with this team and with Coach Albert. You've given your blood, sweat and tears for those guys. You have so many happy memories. Do you really wanna throw that away?" I asked.

"I don't have a choice. Now that Henry's gone, things aren't the same. They'll never be the same again," Ethan grumbled.

I nodded, I understood completely.

"Ms. Salvador, I have proof that Henry sexually assaults girls," Layla declared.

"How?" I asked.

"Beth has polaroids of them half-nude together at a party. Beth says he *raped* her," Layla confessed.

"That's a very serious accusation."

"She said they were hooking up but that she got uncomfortable because of how rough he was being, so she tried to shove him off, but he continued and pinned her down. It's horrible," Layla frowned.

"I knew Henry was an animal but not like that. The way he abused Layla and Beth is just plain evil. I never knew he did this type of shit, and I was his best friend," Ethan shook his head.

"It's okay, Ethan. You didn't know."

"Maybe I should've, mom. I should've known. I couldn't protect the girl I love from him. I failed."

Layla put her arm around his waist and tried to comfort him.

"It's not your fault, baby."

"The past is the past, Ethan. You can reveal who he really is now. Layla can explain her case and try to prove that Henry was a sexual predator," I urged.

"Do you think that'll make the theories worse? It would give us more reason to kill Henry," Ethan said.

"At this point this is a game of truths and lies. The police haven't arrested Layla and they have no reason to. Layla and Beth need to convince the public of Henry's true nature so that they're on their side. They need to tell the better story. That's how we get everyone to forget about the stupid theories."

"You think that'll work?" Ethan asked.

"It's what Lawrence does with his media companies. He tries to tell the better story to convince the public to be on side. He targets and distracts with attention-grabbing headlines. I was friends with him for years when I still talked to Veronica. I saw him do it all the time."

"Okay, I'm ready. I know he's dead, but people need to know what he did to me and to other girls. I don't want him worshipped as some sports hero. Henry's legacy isn't squeaky clean," Layla snapped.

"How do you want them to do it, mom?" Ethan asked.

"Beth and Layla need to get in front of a camera and speak their truth to the world."

I allowed the girls to do it in my house. Beth was a petite girl with long dark hair and a bright sense of style. She wore a yellow cardigan over a white t-shirt with white converse. She had glowing brown eyes, and was as sweet as they came. The thought of Henry abusing her made my blood boil. He knew she was much smaller than her in size. He took that into account. He was a bastard that took advantage.

I had spoken to Willow beforehand, and she was reluctant at first, but she knew that Beth needed to do it, and wanted to do it. So Willow supported her.

The girls set up their phones in front of them on a tripod while they sat on the couch. They pressed record and told their stories. Ethan, Santi, and I watched from behind the camera.

"I don't like speaking ill of the dead, but I felt this needed to be known. Henry Cain sexually assaulted me at a party. I know this comes as a shock and I know a lot of you will probably hate me because he's a murder victim, but it doesn't change who he was. Did he deserve to get murdered? No, of course not. But he wasn't perfect. Yes, he was a star athlete and really popular, but it doesn't change the fact that he sexually abused women," Beth explained.

"Mr. Griffin sexually abused boys and had thousands of files containing child pornography. He was well-liked and look at what he turned out to be. The most infamous sexual predator in our town's history," Layla said.

"You can even argue that because these were well-liked people, they were able to hide their true natures. I'm not saying Henry was on Mr. Griffin's level, but he did rape me. Truthfully, we had planned to hookup at a party. What can I say? I liked him. I really did, but as we began to have sex I started to get really uncomfortable because he started being really rough with me. So, I told him to stop. Many times. I started screaming at him to stop. He put his hand over my mouth and continued on until he finished. He destroyed my sense of self and my inner peace for months. It's only now that I've begun to heal. The reality is, he's dead. So I don't even know how to feel about that. I never wished for him to be dead, but I did want to ask him one question I'll never get to ask him now. Why Henry? Why were you so rough with me? Why didn't you stop when I asked you to? Why didn't you stop when I started screaming?" Beth asked.

"I have a similar story to Beth. My feelings on Henry sexually abusing me were always complicated because he was Ethan's best friend and Ethan is my boyfriend. I thought I could trust Henry and for a while he never tried anything on me until one day in the hall at school he slapped my butt. I was shocked. I didn't know what to do or what to think. He laughed at what he did to me, so I laughed with him. I decided to shrug it off, but that turned out to be a big mistake. I should've told Ethan what was happening much earlier. But I was afraid. I was afraid *he wouldn't believe me because they were like brothers. Eventually it escalated and he started to uh...he started to stick his hand down my pants, and he fingered my privates. This happened on more than one occasion. Like Beth, I didn't wish him dead, and I didn't want revenge. I just wanted to know why?"* Layla asked as she wiped a few tears from her eyes.

"Here's the proof that we hooked up," Beth said as she took out a collection of polaroids that included her and Henry in minimal clothing. They were posing together on a bed.

"I don't have proof that Henry touched me, but I wouldn't lie. I'd never lie about something like that. It happened to Beth, it happened to me, and it happened to other girls who don't want to speak up for their own personal reasons," Layla said.

"We're sorry that Henry's dead and we're sorry that he sexually violated us in horrible ways," Beth said.

"I wanted to get my story out there to let people know that I didn't murder Henry and wouldn't murder him for revenge. I don't have that in me. I haven't been arrested and I haven't been accused of anything because I didn't do it. I was a victim of Henry's sexual abuse. Just because I'm in a picture with him on the day he died doesn't mean I killed him. End of story," Layla concluded.

Beth stopped the recordings. I went over to hug the both of them.

"You guys did great. You got your stories and the truth out there. People will realize what Henry really was. They'll be on your side now," I confidently stated.

"What do you think is gonna happen?" Layla asked.

"Lawrence and Veronica are gonna be really pissed off." I warned.

CHAPTER 16

I was cooking dinner for Ethan, Santi, and Layla when the doorbell rang. My last unexpected visitor was Veronica. I thought about getting Felix's old boxing gloves but decided against it. I had no problem using my bare knuckles against her pointy face. When I opened it, it was actually Omar.

"Oh, hey. What's up?" I asked.

"It smells good in there. What are you cooking?" Omar asked.

"It's a creamy tomato rigatoni with green beans and pesto," I said.

"Damn. That sounds good. I wish I could stay and eat," Omar replied.

"Who said you were invited?" I asked.

"I shouldn't have assumed."

"You're always invited. What are you doing here?" I asked.

"I consider you a good friend, Sonya and that's why I'm here to talk about a video I saw between Ethan and Jonathan," Omar answered.

"Oh boy, come in." I sighed.

Omar walked in and immediately gave an enthusiastic fist bump to Santi who was playing on his computer.

"What's up, little man?" Omar asked.

"Just trying to get through life, Omar," Santi said.

"Damn. He's already going through a teenage crisis?" Omar asked me.

"His brother was arrested and accused of murder. It does things to your mind," I said.

"I'm sorry about that," Omar said.

"I texted him. He'll be down," I said.

A few minutes later, Ethan came skipping down the stairs with disheveled hair and a devilish grin on his face. He shook Omar's hand.

"Where's Layla?" I asked.

"She's sleeping," Ethan said.

"What happened to your hair?" I asked.

"Nothing, mom," Ethan said as he attempted to fix it.

"I don't mean to interrupt your business, young man but I saw the video between you and Jonathan," Omar said.

"That was a friendly scrap. It was nothing serious."

"Don't give him that crap," I scolded.

"What? It's true," Ethan pleaded.

"You guys swung at each other and got into it pretty bad. You also said some pretty terrible things to one another. I came by to tell you that you cannot get into another fight like that. It doesn't look good at all. This is especially bad because Jonathan is a star witness in a big upcoming trial."

"What trial?" Ethan asked.

"Claude Griffin's trial," Omar said.

"Oh shit," Ethan cursed.

"Exactly. So, please be on your best behavior. I don't wanna come here again with handcuffs. Keep your head low, young man."

"Okay, will do," Ethan saluted.

"Yeah and no more rebelling against me or the authorities, okay?" I asked.

"Fine, fine," Ethan mumbled.

"Have you guys seen this?" Layla came downstairs yawning with her phone out.

"No, what is it?" I asked.

"Veronica released a video in response to ours. Lawrence is in it too. It's everywhere. It's on her blog, *Veronica's Vices*," Layla said.

"We'll play it on the TV. Do the phone-connection thing, Ethan," I said.

"That's not what it's called but okay," Ethan managed to get the video playing on the TV and we all watched. Lawrence and Veronica were in their backyard, near their vegetable garden. They had grim expressions on their faces.

"*I am furious. I am very furious,*" Veronica thundered.

"*Yes. I am too,*" Lawrence said.

"*We watched Layla and Beth's ridiculous video accusing my dead son of being a rapist and a sexual abuser. How dare you? How fucking dare you?! He is my son! He is dead! How dare you spoil his good name?! He was not a rapist! He never abused women ever! He was a good, well-behaved boy. My baby boy. He was a great student and an even better athlete. My baby was a star. Henry was a basketball prodigy. Coach Albert would say it all the time. He was meant to do great, big things. He was meant to shoot for the stars. But someone didn't want him there. Someone cruel and evil tragically cut his life short and stole him from us. If that wasn't bad enough, we have two high school sluts staining his good reputation with their lies. Complete and utter lies!"* Veronica screamed.

"Jesus," Omar said under his breath.

"We aren't liars, you crazy lady. Your dead son was a rapist," Layla said coldly.

"We are disgusted and horrified at these allegations and thoroughly reject them. My son was no monster. He was a good human being. To throw these lies over the internet, accusing a dead young boy of horrible crimes is one of the lowest things you can do to another person. He is not even here to defend himself. Shame on you ladies," Lawrence said.

"They're so full of it," Ethan hissed.

"Henry himself was a victim. He was sexually abused by that piece of shit, Griffin. A man he trusted. A man the school trusted to be in charge of children. Henry isn't the abuser, Griffin is. We should be directing all this hate towards him, not my Henry. As the days have gone on and on, I've found it harder and harder to live on without my only child. Every day I wake up crying and every night I go to bed, crying. All I do is think of him. All I hear is his voice. All I want is to hug him again and to love him again," Veronica said.

Despite everything Veronica did to me and everything Henry had done; I couldn't help but feel for her. She was a mother like me and all she wanted was for her child to be in her arms again. I fought hard to prevent myself from shedding tears and lost. I quickly wiped them away.

"I don't get much comfort these days, but there's this noble police officer I know who's a good friend and someone I used to date in college. Felix Salvador spoke to Henry a few hours before he was murdered, and he told me he was in good spirits. I know my baby was...brutally and terribly killed afterwards but at least I knew he was happy at one point during that awful day. I miss him so—," Veronica trailed and couldn't continue as she started weeping. It soon turned to wailing as Lawrence tried to comfort her. The video ended.

"Well that was something," Santi said.

"Felix and Veronica used to date? Did I hear that right?" Omar asked.

"I don't know. They never told me anything like that. They didn't even know each other until I introduced them," I said.

"You think she was lying?" Omar asked.

"Nah, it was probably dad lying. Another one of his secrets," Ethan said.

"If that's true, they both kept it a secret from me," I said.

"What was that about Felix talking to Henry before he was killed?" Layla asked.

"I thought that was weird too," Omar said.

"I sense a lot of weird shit going on," Ethan said.

Ethan was right. Why was Felix talking to Henry just hours before he was murdered? Why did he lie about seeing him that day? Why didn't Felix and Veronica tell me they used to date back then? What else were they hiding from me? Did Felix cheat on me with her throughout my entire marriage?

Before I could think further about any of those questions, we all heard a loud banging outside my house that grew louder and louder. It sounded like water droplets, but it wasn't raining. When I peeked outside the front window, I saw a fast-moving object hurling towards me. I ducked out of the way as a massive brick broke through and shattered the window, spilling shards of glass everywhere.

I yelled at Ethan, Santi, and Layla to get down on the ground. Omar pulled out his gun and rushed to my side. I looked outside for a brief second and saw two black cars. It was them again. They had come back.

"What the hell is going on?" Omar asked urgently.

"It's them Omar! The people who attacked my house last time!"

I flinched as I heard multiple large objects being lobbed at my front door.

"I think they're throwing more bricks. Are these people insane?" Omar asked.

Ethan murdered Henry Cain! Accept the truth!
Henry was a good kid! He never deserved to die!
Long live Henry!

Several voices rang out. They sounded young. Omar got up and dashed outside with his gun raised. He pointed it at the black cars as they screeched away. He fired one bullet that crackled through the air and penetrated one of their sideview mirrors. I ran to the children and made sure they were okay.

"Are you guys hurt? No one got hit right?" I asked.

"We're okay," Ethan said.

"Just a little shaken up. That was scary. I thought they were shooting at us," Layla shuddered.

"It's the same idiots who threw rocks last time," I scoffed.

"Who are they, mom?" Santi asked.

"I wish I knew honey," I said.

"Are you alright, mom?" Ethan asked.

I noticed that I was shaking, and my heart was thumping fast. I sat down and tried to relax.

"Yeah, I'll be fine," I said.

"I got their plates. I'll track them down," Omar said.

"Thank you, Omar."

"You got someone to fix your broken window?" Omar asked.

"I'll call someone in the morning," I said.

"Don't worry guys. It'll all be okay. Let's try to keep cool heads," Omar urged.

"Sounds like a good idea."

"You should throw bricks at those fuckers when you catch them, Omar!" Santi exclaimed.

"Santi, watch your language."

"I'm sorry, I couldn't help it."

We all laughed a bit, trying to shake off the scary event we had just experienced. After reassuring Layla's parents on the phone that my house was safe and that we weren't being targeted by domestic terrorists, I tried my best to sleep after an eventful night. My mind had other ideas. I experienced the recurring nightmare yet again. I tripped and fell out of an open window.

As I slowly tumbled down, I saw the old man below me inches away from hitting the ground. When he did, I fell on top of him. All his blood and guts stuck to my face and my body like red glue. I tasted bits of his bloodied brain mixed together with his shattered skull. I screamed.

When I woke up in the middle of that awful night, I grabbed my pillow and buried my face in it. I cried and cried until there were no more tears left. I needed to let it all out before it consumed me. I was having a nightmare during the day and at night. I had no escape. It was getting harder and harder to keep myself together.

CHAPTER 17

Things calmed down a bit after my house was attacked. Omar was busily tracking down the people who did it and the window was being fixed. Thankfully it was the weekend. I was waiting for the boys to get ready to go to their dad's house. I needed to speak to Felix about the whole dating situation with Veronica in college. I needed things cleared up. From what I understood, they never knew each other until I started dating Felix and introduced them. I couldn't stomach any more lies.

BEFORE

I first met Veronica in an auditorium class. The subject was philosophy. I was late that day and was forced to sit towards the back. There was an open seat next to a young, thin blonde doing her makeup. It was Veronica Cain. The rest was history.

"Oh my god, I love your shoes," Veronica said.

"Oh, thanks. I like yours too," I said.

"They could be better."

"Oh, I guess so," I said.

"I'm Veronica Cain. You?"

"I'm Sonya Guerra."

"Are you new?" Veronica asked.

"Oh no. I've been here the whole semester. I never sit in the back. I'm always in the front, but I was late today," I said.

"You wouldn't catch me dead sitting in the front. I need privacy when I do my makeup."

I noticed that she had her laptop open, but it was dark. It wasn't even on. She didn't have any notebooks out either.

"You don't come to class to study?" I asked.

"Oh, god no. What even is this class? Chemistry? I don't even know what that is," Veronica laughed.

"It's philosophy, I find it interesting. I wanna be a teacher," I said.

"A teacher? God bless you, girl. I could never," Veronica said.

"How come?"

"The salary is way too low," Veronica said.

"You're not wrong, but I really wanna teach kids," I said.

"You'll get bored of it and eventually hate it. All teachers do," Veronica said.

She turned out to be right, to a degree. I didn't hate it, but it got tougher to rekindle the passion I had for it year after year. The system wore you down after a while.

"We'll see what happens," I said.

"I'm gonna be rich," Veronica gloated.

"What do you major in?" I asked.

"I don't even remember. I plan to marry rich, sweetheart," Veronica said.

"Oh."

I found it so odd when she said that. I couldn't believe anyone would marry someone just for money. I later learned the idea wasn't so far-fetched. People married other people for money reasons all the time. They just never revealed the truth.

"There's this guy named Lawrence Whitlock. He is filthy rich. I'm talking downright disgusting, Sonya. I will marry him, and I will enjoy his money," Veronica said.

"Is he a student?" I asked.

"Hell no," Veronica giggled.

"What is he?"

"He's a businessman. He works in media and news. He gives lectures here on campus about business a few times a year. He's an alma mater or whatever," Veronica said.

"Sounds like an interesting man. When did he graduate?" I asked.

"A while ago, he's like forty."

I almost fell off my seat when she said that.

"You mean 40 years old?"

"Yep. He's a daddy."

"He can be *your* daddy."

Veronica gaped at me and playfully hit my arm.

"You bitch! You are not funny," Veronica gasped.

We stared at each other until we giggled so hard we had to cover our mouths so we wouldn't disrupt the class.

"You got me good, Sonya. You got me good."

"I didn't mean it," I said.

"I can take a joke. I don't care."

"That's good. Your new daddy will like that."

"He better. I'm trying to live a good life. I don't wanna struggle. I've struggled my whole life. Trust me, being poor sucks. It sucks really hard. I've been poor since I was born. I'm trying to change my future. My life was not destined to be tragic," Veronica said.

It struck me hard in my heart when she said that. I thought that she was insane for marrying Lawrence at such a young age when he was so much older, but I quietly understood where she was coming from. She didn't want to struggle anymore. I connected with that. We became fast friends after that. Things were great between us once. I even looked at her like a sister. It was a shame it all eventually came crashing down.

PRESENT DAY

Santi came into my room and locked the door. He slid on to my bed and came close to me with serious eyes.

"I have to tell you something, mom. It's about Ethan," Santi said.

"What is it, honey?" I asked.

"Before Henry died, I saw Ethan in his room with a box cutter," Santi revealed.

"You saw him with what?"

"A box cutter. The murder weapon. I heard about it from the other kids in school. The ones who won't leave me alone."

"Did you ask him why he had that box cutter?"

"Yeah, he told me if I said anything about it to anyone he would die. So I didn't say anything, but now I'm scared. The house was attacked and there's all these Reddit theories that are saying Ethan and Layla killed Henry together for revenge. I don't want Ethan to go to prison, mom. I don't want him to get arrested again. Why do you think he had that box cutter?" Santi asked.

My heart pounded against my chest as I thought about the implications of what Santi told me. Why did Ethan have a box cutter? Why did he tell Santi he was gonna die if he told anyone? It wasn't normal behavior for a 16-year-old. I needed to know the truth immediately.

"I'm not sure, Santi. I'm gonna ask him. Just keep what you told me to yourself. Everything is gonna be okay. I promise you."

"Okay, mom. I'll wait downstairs to go to dad's house," Santi ran out of the room.

I hated making promises I wasn't sure I could keep, but I couldn't have said anything else. I needed Santi to remain calm. He was far too young to be stressed out about those sorts of things.

I barged into Ethan's room and found him at his desk on his computer. He was looking at Lawrence's ridiculous media propaganda that had his face on it. They had him photoshopped with an orange jumpsuit and blood on his hands. Another picture had him holding a bloody knife. **DEATH PENALTY** was written at the top as well as **JUSTICE FOR HENRY CAIN**.

"Mom?"

"Yes?"

"Why is Lawrence Whitlock calling for my death?" Ethan asked.

"I don't know, but I'm gonna have a talk with him. I'll make him end this ridiculous media crusade. It's gone on long enough," I said as my voice shook with anger.

My skin felt like it was about to erupt into flames. Someone was calling for the *death* of *my son*. Someone who had been released by the police. Someone who was, by all accounts, *innocent* of the terrible crime he had been accused of. I had the nerve to drive my car into his house to destroy it. Hopefully he would get hit and die on impact. You do not wish death upon my innocent child. I knew he was in great pain and sorrow because of Henry's death but Ethan had nothing to do with it. End of story.

"Are you sure? He's rich."

"I don't care. I'll tell him off. We used to be friends. He's not that scary."

"Well in that case let's carpet bomb his house," Ethan joked.

"I don't have the power to do that, but I will make him stop," I said.

"Mom, do you think they'll arrest me again? I'm worried because Omar saw me fight Jonathan. I can't believe someone got it on video."

"You have to remember the era we live in. Everyone has their phones out. It's very easy to record anything that happens nowadays. You should know that more than anyone," I said.

"I guess."

"Is this why you don't wanna go back to school?"

"It's part of the reason. What if other kids start bothering me like they bother Santi? I won't lie mom, I don't wanna deal with that. I think I might as well transfer now."

"It's too late in the year. You'll fall behind in your classes. We'll talk about it this summer," I said.

"Fine."

"What about Layla? You're gonna leave her?" I asked.

"She's coming with me. I talked to her about it," Ethan said.

"She must really love you."

"I love her too. She's everything to me, mom. I'd do anything for her. I'd kill for her," Ethan stated.

"Would you now?" I asked.

"It's an expression. You know what I mean," Ethan said.

I nodded and mentally prepared myself to answer the question that had been on my mind since I walked through the door.

"Ethan, I have to ask you a serious question," I said.

"What's up?"

"Santi told me he saw you with a box cutter before Henry got murdered. Is that true?" I asked.

Ethan squirmed in his seat.

"Hello?" I asked.

"Are we really doing this?"

"Ethan, answer the question."

"Santi has such a big mouth," Ethan grumbled.

"Ethan, *answer the question.*"

"Yes, yes I had one."

"Why on earth did you have Mr. Griffin's box cutter?"

Ethan looked at me and laughed in my face. I wanted to slap him but refrained from hitting him. I always stopped myself. I didn't want to be like my father. My children will never be afraid of me.

"This is no laughing matter, Ethan. You're worrying me."

Ethan turned around and reached into his desk drawer. He promptly pulled out a box cutter. It was yellow.

"It wasn't Mr. Griffin's box cutter. It was mine. I use it to open packages I buy online. It's mostly basketball jerseys and stuff. I was messing with Santi."

I breathed out a sigh of relief. It was a false alarm. I always wanted to believe that my son was innocent, but in the nagging dark corners of my mind were little voices that told me to think otherwise. Little voices that told me Ethan had all the reasons in the world to murder his best friend.

"I'm sorry, I was just making sure. I didn't know you had one."

Ethan stared at me for the longest time with a frown. I wasn't sure what to do or say so I just waited. I could tell many things that concerned him were running through his mind. The air between us was charged with sheer awkwardness and confusion. He looked at me like I was a stranger.

"Do you think I murdered Henry?" Ethan whispered.

"No, of course not. I would never think that," I said.

"If you really believed me, you wouldn't be asking me if I had a knife," Ethan snapped.

"I'm your mother. I was just making sure," I said.

"You were making sure that I didn't kill him, I get it."

"Ethan, it's not like that."

"You don't trust me."

"Of course I trust you, honey," I said as I placed my hand on his. He angrily slipped it off. A sharp stabbing sensation instantly pierced my heart.

"Whatever mom," Ethan sighed as he stood up.

"Ethan, I trust you."

He went towards the door and opened it. He held it and motioned for me to leave. I slowly did so, and he slammed it shut. I couldn't believe it.

"Ethan! I do trust you and I love you more than anything. You have to know that," I urged.

Silence. I decided to let him be and to let him cool off. I put myself in his shoes. How upset would I be if my mother thought I was capable of murdering someone?

Ethan didn't speak to me during the entire ride to Felix's house. When he got there, he hopped out of my car and slammed the door shut.

"It's okay, mom. He'll get over it. He's kind of mad at me too," Santi said.

"I hope so, Santi. I love you."

"Love you too."

Felix greeted them on his front lawn and ushered them inside. He waited for me to get out.

"I got your message, Sonya. Can we make this quick? I'm watching the game and got a hot date with an ice-cold beer," Felix said.

"That's cute."

"Oh boy, you're angry. I can already tell. Are you about to go on a rampage?" Felix asked.

"You're a piece of shit liar."

"Okay, you've said this before. You already know what I am."

"Did you see Lawrence and Veronica's video?" I asked.

"No, but I heard about it. She mentioned me," Felix said.

"Yeah, she mentioned that you two dated. Is that true?" I asked.

"Does it even matter now?" Felix asked.

"Are you serious? You never told me. That's such a strange secret to keep," I said.

"It's not a strange secret. Veronica and I knew you would probably act like this."

"You know I'm not like that."

"She became your best friend. You would've gotten jealous. It would've ruined your friendship," Felix said.

"You two ruined it anyway," I snapped.

"Life sucks sometimes, Sonya," Felix mocked.

"Who's idea was it to keep it a secret?" I asked.

"It was hers. Look, she just wanted to keep things civil, and she didn't think it was worth bringing up. We only dated for a couple of months. It meant nothing," Felix said.

"If it meant nothing then why didn't you tell me? You acted like you two didn't even know each other when I introduced you to her," I said.

I remembered it as clear as day. I told Veronica about Felix who was a cop and she acted like she had no idea who he was. That bitch was a bold-faced liar.

"I don't know what to tell you, Sonya. It was ages ago," Felix said.

"You could've told me the truth," I stated.

"You can't handle the truth. You never could," Felix said.

"Like what?" I asked.

"Never mind. This is a pointless conversation," Felix yawned.

"What? That you loved her? That you've always loved her? Even during our marriage? Was it all a lie?" I asked.

"Don't go there. She left me for Lawrence's money. What do you think?"

"I think you do love her. You cheated on me with her. So there's that," I said.

"You're insufferable."

I stomped closer to him.

"Why? Why Felix? Why did you pick me? Huh? I want to know why. Why did you approach me back in college? Why did you date me, knowing that you still loved Veronica?" I asked.

He couldn't even look me in the eyes. He puffed out a sigh.

"You were a beautiful woman and you looked incapable of breaking my heart."

I was taken aback by his honest response. After all those years, I finally knew the truth.

"So I was your rebound after she dumped you. That's incredible," I said.

"It wasn't like that."

"Of course it was. I'm not an idiot, Felix. Please stop treating me like one."

"She wanted this you know. She knew you were gonna watch that video and she dropped that little line like a grenade. She always egged us on to fight. The shit with Omar...she loved the drama."

"I have no problem giving her a show."

"I think you do have a problem. I told you. You can't handle the truth."

"*Screw your truth,*" I barked.

"You can't handle that truth and the truth about our son," Felix said.

"What the hell are you talking about?" I asked.

"The truth that Ethan murdered Henry because he was jealous of him. He was jealous that he was the better player."

"You're insane. How can you think that of your own son?" I asked.

"The truth hurts. I saw that video of Ethan fighting Jonathan Locke at *Moe's*. I also saw the one of him fighting Henry during practice. He can't control himself, Sonya. The kid's got issues. He's violent. He has impulses," Felix shrugged his shoulders.

You're violent too and you're his father.

I didn't dare to say it out loud. I didn't want that connection between Ethan and his father to be real. Ethan turning out violent because of Felix? It would've destroyed me. It couldn't be true. I would not accept that.

"I can't believe you're saying all that," I said.

"Maybe we don't know who our son really is, Sonya."

"*Maybe you don't know because you were never there for him! But I do know! I know who my son is! Don't you dare pretend to know who he is! How could you?! You didn't raise him! I did!*" I shouted.

I couldn't hold it in anymore. The obvious hate and resentment that Felix had for his own son had reached its boiling point with me. I wouldn't tolerate it anymore. I was ready to explode. I shoved him back with all the force I had inside of me and stepped backwards before I did anything else I would regret.

"Don't you dare touch me, Sonya. Remember what happened last time?" Felix asked with darkened eyes.

"How could I forget? It was the day I realized you were the most pathetic, cowardly man I had ever met."

"You say all that, but you were married to that man for 10 years," Felix said.

"And somehow I survived."

"You keep telling yourself that."

"I will," I said as I went back to my car and furiously drove off.

I said just about every single curse word under my breath as I dried my watery eyes. Omar called me shortly afterwards and I did my best to mask my strained voice.

"*Hey Omar,*" I said.

"*I know who attacked your house, Sonya. I think it's some kids Lawrence hired to spook you,*" Omar said.

"*How do you know?*"

"*I snooped around your old college and started asking questions. Lawrence is known for hiring college boys to do things like that. He gives business lectures there,*" Omar said.

"*I'm gonna kill him.*"

"*I can handle this.*"

"*No, I'll handle this. I need to do this myself.*"

"*Are you sure? I don't think that's a good idea,*" Omar said.

"*Omar, I'm doing this,*" I said.

"*Alright, Sonya. Just make sure you call me the minute it goes south,*" Omar said.

"*It won't.*"

I met Lawrence at his favorite coffee shop. It was a trendy, uppity place. The interior consisted of exposed brick walls, minimalist furniture, and warm lighting that casted a cozy glow, giving off an ambiance that was calm and peaceful. Lawrence had told me back then that he used to take business partners there when he wanted to cut ties with them. He would rip apart their hopes and dreams while sipping on a cinnamon latte macchiato with almond milk. Lawrence always dressed like he was about to step into an important business meeting. He wore a charcoal grey jacket with a finely pressed, pristine white dress shirt perfectly tucked underneath. He had on a pair of expertly tailored trousers with a slight break at the ankle. I made sure not to step on his polished leather oxfords that gleamed with a glossy sheen. I imagined him going to sleep with that outfit on.

"Hello Sonya. It's been a while."

"Hi Lawrence."

"We both know why we're here so why don't we cut to the chase? I have no interest or patience in talking niceties."

You haven't changed one bit. Dick.

"I know you attacked my house on two separate occasions. You had college kids in black cars pelt my house with rocks and bricks. Very juvenile of you."

"I have no idea what you're talking about."

"I know it was you," I firmly stated.

"I'm sorry your house was attacked but I had nothing to do with that."

"Fine, I can't prove that, but I can prove that you're calling for the death penalty against my son when he isn't even in police custody anymore."

"How can you prove that?" Lawrence asked.

"Don't play dumb. It was produced by one of your media companies. It's not hard to find."

"I'm just going by the facts. The murder weapon was found in your son's locker, and he had Henry's blood on his hands," Lawrence said.

"The blood results were inconclusive," I said.

"Everyone knows it was Henry's blood."

"You're not making any sense."

Lawrence drank a sip of his coffee and sighed. His expression seemed to soften as he briefly closed his eyes. He looked like he was in pain and Lawrence wasn't the type of man to showcase his suffering. He looked like he would keep it in for all time until his death.

"I can't do it anymore," Lawrence said.

"What?" I asked.

"I can't do this whole song and dance anymore. I'm tired. I'm really tired," Lawrence sighed.

"We don't have to, Lawrence. I get it. Everything's different now," I said.

"I haven't been getting a lot of sleep since Henry's death," Lawrence admitted.

"I understand."

"You know what keeps me up at night?" Lawrence asked.

"What?" I asked.

"The fact that I may have failed him as a father. That video that Layla and Beth released made everything a hundred times worse."

"That was their truth, Lawrence. They had to tell their side of the story. Just like how you told yours."

"You have to understand why we made and uploaded that response, Sonya. When we heard what Layla and Beth said, we were beyond angry. We felt absolute rage and wrath in our souls. We couldn't believe that Henry was being accused of sexual assault and other horrible things. Henry was our son, Sonya. What would you do if Ethan was accused of those things?" Lawrence asked.

"I would hope that I would never be in that situation, but he was accused of murder and arrested. I know how you're feeling, trust me. You and Veronica will get through it," I said.

"Veronica isn't like you. She's spiraling. She's losing it, Sonya. You're a tough woman. You've survived a lot of hardship and you fight back. Veronica may do it on the outside, but on the inside—she's already dead. She has been for a while. She doesn't sleep, she barely eats, and she spends all her time grieving Henry," Lawrence said.

"Oh Veronica. As a mother, I understand. It's impossible, Lawrence. She needs a lot of time," I said.

"Do you really think Henry was capable of those things? You can be honest with me. I need to know."

"I'm sorry Lawrence, but I believe Layla and Beth. I saw Henry physically assaulting Layla with my own eyes. I even spoke to Principal Jacobson about it. He had a problem, Lawrence. I don't know why or how it came about, but he treated girls very badly."

"I only have myself to blame. I should've been a better father. I guess I was too tired with work and too old to really pay attention to what he was doing. I turned a blind eye, Sonya. He would bring different girls to his room almost every week. It wasn't normal behavior. I saw the way he treated them. The way he would manhandle them. I've been lying to myself his entire life."

That was news to me. Lawrence changed after Henry's death. It was inevitable. That was his only son. It would drive any parent mad. He seemed more reflective and guilt-ridden because of what happened. The way he dressed on the outside masked what he felt on the inside.

"Maybe we shouldn't have had him. I don't know. Veronica and I have such a large age gap. I tried to convince myself that it didn't matter but of course it mattered. It's most likely why she slept with Felix after so many years."

"I believe so too."

"I'm sorry about that. We're both victims of that very unfortunate situation."

"How did you ever forgive her for that?"

"There was many reasons. I wanted to stay together because of Henry and because I wanted to stay married. She said it was the worst decision of her life. I wasn't giving her much attention because of work so I partly blamed myself. We had a good life, and I didn't want to throw it away. However, I did tell her that if she ever cheated again, our marriage was over, our life together was over and that I would take everything from her. I have the money and the resources to ensure that she never gets a penny from me in a potential divorce and if Henry was still around, she'd never see him again," Lawrence revealed.

"You're far more forgiving than I am," I said.

"Everyone has their limits," Lawrence said.

"I have to ask you something, did you know Felix and Veronica dated?" I asked.

"I had a feeling, but I never bothered to ask for the longest time. She told me a couple of years ago. They had a couple of polaroids together from old college frat parties." Lawrence said.

"They never told me, ever. I don't understand the lying or the secrecy. I don't care that they dated. It's the fact that they never told me and then ended up sleeping with each other which destroyed my marriage completely," I said.

"Everyone has their reasons, Sonya. That's what I've learned. Maybe they planned it. Maybe they slept with each other during the entirety of both of our marriages," Lawrence said.

"How did we all used to be so close? I was best friends with Veronica. We were pregnancy pals. Ethan and Henry were best friends and now he's gone. Nothing will ever be the same," I sighed.

"It's a never-ending nightmare."

As I entered my car, it felt like what we all had wasn't even real. After Henry's death, all the lies and secrets we all had spilled out. It exposed everything that never was. I questioned everything. My marriage, my children, my friends, my profession, and my entire life. Was I the same as them? Was I the same as Felix, Veronica, and Lawrence? Was I purposely turning a blind eye to who I really was?

The thought pounded in my head.

We all lie to save ourselves.

My eyes darted erratically around the dashboard as my breaths became shallow and rapid. My body trembled as I clutched the steering wheel in a desperate attempt to keep myself stable. My vision grew hazy as my mind was enveloped in a fog of wildly negative thoughts and dark memories that were formed during my tumultuous childhood. I struggled to keep a grip on reality, but I was failing, and I wasn't sure what to do next. I considered just driving but I quickly realized that would end in a terribly tragic accident. My phone rang and my head whiplashed forward, banging it on the wheel. While I groaned and massaged my head, I answered the call. It was Omar.

"Sonya, we need to talk."

Thankfully my mental breakdown ended when Omar called. Henry's murder, Ethan's behavior, Felix's lies, Veronica's secrets and Lawrence's revelations all took its toll on me. It came out in the worst way possible, but I was determined to fight through it. I had to. There was no way out. I had to cut right through the darkness and come out the other side alive.

The day had turned cool, and a windy breeze traveled through the quiet park which was completely devoid of people. The sun was setting and projecting it's golden rays across the landscape. I took a neatly paved pathway to sit next to Omar, who was situated on a steel bench.

"How was your meeting with Lawrence?"

"It was productive. We caught up. He agreed to stop the smear campaigns against my son," I said.

"He shouldn't have done it in the first place. Imagine you're a teenager and you're seeing online that you deserve the death penalty. What is that?"

"You don't understand how pissed off I was when I saw it," I said.

"Things feel like they should've gotten better by now but nothing's changed. We've hit a snag in Henry's case. We were really gunning for Griffin to be the murderer."

"That's completely out the window?"

"There's no way he did it. It doesn't add up. He was all the way on the other side of town. There's no way to pinpoint him anywhere near Blackwood Forest during the estimated time of Henry's murder."

"I thought it was him too. I don't know who else it could be."

"I do."

"Who?"

"Sonya...do you think it's possible that Felix murdered Henry?"

I remained dead silent while I processed the gravity of what he had asked me. I had thought about it of course, in theory, but was Felix capable of murdering a teenage boy? He loved Henry so the whole idea felt very alien in nature. But the facts remained.

"He told me he didn't see him on the day he died but then Veronica said that they spoke on the day he died."

"We spoke with him again. He admitted to it. He was in contact with him just a few hours before he was murdered. He supposedly spoke to him privately at school about basketball then went back to work."

"Then there's his blood being on the box cutter. I don't buy his excuse. How do you mishandle a sharp knife in an evidence locker?"

"He's your ex-husband. What do you think?"

"Once a liar, always a liar."

"Felix's story does keep changing and it's concerning. I just don't see why he would do it. He had a good relationship with the kid. I can't see how everything went wrong in the span of a few hours."

"I'm surprised he hasn't been arrested yet."

"He's a cop. It's unfortunate, but you know how it is. My bosses are reluctant. They won't touch him unless they're 100 percent certain he did it."

"I have a horrible feeling that this whole thing is not gonna end well."

"I feel it too. It's the calm before the storm. Hopefully we're wrong," Omar said.

"I have a feeling Henry may have found out something about him, that he didn't want to get out. Something so terrible that Felix had to murder him," I said.

CHAPTER 18
28 YEARS AGO

I didn't have the best childhood. I lived in a household built on chaos, arguments, and anger. My father was the main culprit. A haggard, bad-tempered man with scraggly hair and bloodshot eyes. He was a force of wrath who dished out punishment to my mother and I on a regular basis. He would find reasons to abuse us and sometimes he would give no reason at all.

My mother used work as a way to combat the pain and misery we were living in. I had nothing but my own dark, violent thoughts to dwell in as the years went by. We lived in a derelict house with walls that had peeling paint, cracked windows and a sagging roof that looked like it would collapse at any second. The front lawn was overgrown with weeds and vines taking over the driveway. The wooden front door had scratches and was rotting. The flooring was damaged and creaked every time you stepped on it.

My house was one of squalor and neglect. We didn't have happy days. My parents argued constantly about the state of their finances and there wasn't much food in the kitchen, ever. Dad was a general handyman and would get jobs when he felt like it. He spent most of his time drinking until he passed out.

Mom was the one who tried to keep us together and sane. She had a job at a restaurant as a dishwasher. She worked like a horse. She would go day, night, weekends, holidays, almost every day to keep us afloat. She tried. She really did. What did she get for it? She got nothing she deserved. She got hell. We both did. That was the day everything changed. That was the day I realized that I was truly alone in the world.

I quietly sat near my father while he drank, and I did homework. He was watching a gambling show on TV.

"Dad, can you help me?" I asked.

"No, leave me alone," Dad grumbled.

"Okay."

That was his typical answer. I didn't know why I even tried. Mom was the only one who helped me. I was happy when she came home. It meant I didn't have to be near that deadbeat anymore. She was coming from work and looked absolutely exhausted.

"Hey sweetie," Mom said.

Mom was a lean, strong woman who still had the brightness in her eyes even after everything she had been through with that evil man.

"Hi Mom!" I said running up to her and giving her a hug. I was only 7 years old. I still had my innocence. I still believed that things would somehow get better.

"Hey Vic," Mom said.

"How was work?" Dad asked.

"Tiring as hell," Mom sighed.

"I bet," Dad said.

"Did you get anything lined up?" Mom asked.

"Not yet, I still gotta call some people," Dad said.

"You can't do that now?" Mom asked.

"Don't start with me, Sienna. I'm in a good mood," Dad said.

"You're always in a good mood, apparently," Mom said.

"What the hell did you say to me?" Dad asked.

He rose from his worn-out couch chair and sized up my mom. I slipped out of the way and watched from a distance as I felt a sharp pain in the pit of my stomach.

"I don't want to do this now, Vic. I'm tired and I wanna go to sleep," Mom mumbled.

"If you don't wanna start it, don't be saying dumb shit then," Dad snapped.

"Whatever, Vic," Mom sighed.

Dad examined her up and down. He shook his head and threw a plate from the kitchen on the floor, shattering it.

"What the hell is your problem?!" Mom shouted.

"Why are you wearing your shirt out like that? You're showing everything. You're showing your boobs. You have a boyfriend at work or something?" Dad asked.

"No, Vic. It's hot. Lord forgive me for showing a little cleavage," Mom shook her head.

"This isn't the first time you've done this shit," Dad said with darkened eyes.

"I'm in my own house. I don't see what the problem is. You're being ridiculous," Mom said.

When she tried to walk away, he savagely gripped her throat and started choking her. She struggled to breathe and clawed at his hands, desperately trying to get free. After a few more fateful seconds, he let go and shoved her hard to the floor. *Thud.* She violently coughed. I wanted to go to her side badly, but he was there. He would've done the same to me.

"What the hell, Vic? I did nothing to you," Mom croaked.

"You're behaving like a stupid whore. That's what you're doing!" Dad yelled.

"Go to hell," Mom cried with tears running down her face.

I saw the blood rushing to Dad's face as he grabbed Mom's ponytail and started dragging her upstairs despite her impassioned protesting. I sneakily followed them up and saw that he took her inside their bedroom. The door was left a tad bit open. I peeked through the crack and saw Dad punching Mom in the stomach while she clutched it and groaned in pain. *Thwack. Thwack. Thwack. Thwack. Thwack.* When she tried to stop him with her hand, he viciously slapped her across the face and stomped her knee down to the floor. She howled in pain.

"Don't you ever get tired of doing this to me?" Mom cried.

"Stop talking, you deserve it," Dad growled.

"Vic, please. All I want is to go to sleep. Please let me go to sleep," Mom pleaded.

"I need to teach you a lesson again," Dad threatened.

He grabbed her by her ponytail and dragged her to the window. She tried to use her feet to dig into the floor to stop him, but he kicked her legs away and briefly pulled her head, severely hurting her. He opened the window and prepared to pick her up. She fought tooth and nail to escape him.

"No! No! Vic, no! Stop it! Stop it right now! Let me go! What the hell are you doing?!" Mom shrieked.

"Stop moving!" Vic shouted.

I was petrified but I had to help Mom. I had to move. I swallowed the lump that had accumulated in my throat and dashed forward. I started punching Dad's hands, but it wasn't working. He powerfully backhanded me and I went flying.

"No! Don't touch her! Don't touch my baby!" Mom yelled.

"Don't fucking tell me what to do!" Vic boomed.

I hurt my tailbone when I crashed to the floor and wanted to cry. I felt defeated. I saw that Dad was succeeding and that Mom was slowly giving up. She had no more energy left to give.

If I don't help her. She will die. My mommy will die. I thought.

I forced myself to get up and ran back towards him. I opened my mouth and bit down hard on his fingers. He flinched back in pain and yelped. Mom was free. She crawled away from him. She wrapped herself around me as my father stumbled back and was halfway out through the window. He had both arms outstretched, barely holding onto the ledge.

"Help me! Help me! I'm gonna fall! Come on!" Dad bellowed.

I glanced at Mom and saw that she was blank faced. She didn't move a muscle. I got out of her hold and sprinted to Dad.

"Yeah that's it. Come on! I'm slipping! Sienna help me! What the fuck are you doing?! I'm gonna fall! I'm gonna fucking fall you stupid bitch!"

As I glanced at Dad and at Mom, I made a split-second decision. I barely thought it. I just...acted. It was pure instinct, pure survival mode. I leaned forward...and pushed him. He fell backwards with a terror-stricken look on his face and a fear-inducing scream that punctured the quiet air like a siren.

I didn't look away as his body crashed the harsh pavement below and exploded. Dark blood oozed from underneath as bits and pieces of his brain and skull scattered his surroundings. His arms and legs were bent in very unnatural directions. He was dead. There was no doubt about it. I murdered Dad. I pushed him...and killed him.

It wasn't an accident. I meant to do it. That's what scared me the most about myself. I was a murderer. Mom came over and looked out the window. She saw what was left of Dad and gasped. She crouched down to my eye level and gripped my shoulders.

"It was an accident. If anyone asks, it was an accident. You will never speak of what you did. Do you understand me?" Mom asked.

"Yes Mom," I nodded.

"I'm sorry, Sonya. I'm so sorry. I'm so sorry that our life has been nothing, but tragic," Mom said as she pulled me in, and wailed.

Things were never the same again. It became my darkest secret. I murdered my own father. Dad's death was ruled an accident, and we went about our lives. We were no longer abused and beaten. We were no longer victims. We were just people who tried to live in peace while we tightly held our darkest secret deep in our hearts.

Mom was fairly mute after Dad's death. She didn't like to talk much and never talked about Dad. She never said it, but I knew she was happy that he was gone. She didn't miss him trying to throw her out of a second-story window for showing cleavage. I didn't miss him disrupting my peace and beating me to half-death. He used to leave me marks and other bruises.

He needed to be gone. I didn't know how I knew that as a 7-year-old, but I just did. What worried me most about being a murderer was being a mother to Ethan. Did he have the same violent instinct I had? If Felix and I both had violence in our DNA, was it passed down to Ethan? Since I was capable of murdering my father, would Ethan be capable of murdering his best friend?

Did I secretly know the truth all along? Was I lying to save myself?

CHAPTER 19
PRESENT DAY

I remembered that it was my father's birthday. I always remembered that I had killed him on his birthday. That day was no different. That day everything changed forever. I was working on a lesson plan after school while waiting for a reply back from Ethan. I had sent him about thousand texts. He was still ignoring me. He was still upset about what I had asked him, and I wasn't sure how to fix it. I just kept trying to reach him and hoped he would answer soon.

When I heard a ring I got excited and lunged for my phone. I was slightly disappointed when it was Willow. She needed me in her office. It seemed serious. I passed Mr. Griffin's room as I made my way to her office. It was completely emptied out and had a heavy lock on the door. My stomach churned just thinking about him. Mr. Griffin's evil spirit lived in that room. The horrific crimes he committed and all the innocent lives he destroyed would never be forgotten.

When I entered Willow's office, Omar was there. They were both standing with solemn expressions. The air in the room was ice cold, and charged with dread. A shiver ran down my spine.

"What's going on?" I asked.

"We wanted to tell you this before you heard it somewhere else," Willow said.

"Veronica has been missing for two days. Lawrence reported it," Omar said.

"Jesus, what happened?" I asked.

"He said he doesn't know," Omar said.

"He's lying," I snapped.

"He definitely is. He won't tell us what happened," Omar replied.

"This is strange. I have a bad feeling about this," I uttered.

"Me too. Considering her son died, this is highly concerning. Who knows what she's doing?" Willow asked.

"You know her better than anyone. Where could she have gone?" Omar asked.

"Did you try Felix's house?" I asked.

"I already swung by, she's not there. He's spearheading the search. They're checking the whole town," Omar said.

"She's really missing," I whispered.

"Her phone's dead and her car's gone," Omar revealed.

"Do you think she just wanted to leave Lawrence and disappear?" Willow asked.

"Has she used any credit cards or anything?" I asked.

"None yet," Omar said.

"I don't know, Willow. I don't think she'd leave him. If she chose to leave him that means she chose to leave the money. She would never," I said.

"Maybe it's something else. Maybe she found out about something," Omar said.

"Like what?" Willow asked.

"Maybe she realized Henry really was a sexual predator and is having a mental breakdown somewhere," I said.

"She's been gone two whole days. Where the hell could she be?" Willow asked.

Omar's phone rang and he read a text message he received. Omar's eyes bulged as he bolted towards the door.

"What happened?" I asked.

"Veronica's car has been found by a hiking trail near Blackwood Forest. I'm joining the search," Omar declared.

"I'll go with you."

It was pouring hard as we hopped out of Omar's police cruiser, and trekked through the muddy ground, into the forest. The raincoats we put on did little to shield us from the thick droplets that pummeled us relentlessly from above. The brooding, stormy sky turned everything into a shade of gray. We were shrouded in a watery curtain as we did our best to avoid soaking our shoes in rapidly forming puddles.

"Are we near them?" I asked.

"No. We're on the opposite side. We'll meet in the middle," Omar answered.

We crossed from tree to tree, taking refuge underneath the flurry of branches to have a temporary retreat from the onslaught of water that didn't want to let up. Eventually we reached a small cliff and descended it.

We saw a silhouetted figure in the distance amongst the bushes and foliage. It looked like the outline of a person. As we got closer and closer I dropped to my knees. It was a losing struggle to control the ferocious turbulence in my stomach as my shoulder lurched forward, ready to empty out the contents of my agitated belly.

When I glanced back up, I immediately puked into a muddy puddle and quickly wiped my mouth. I slowly stood up and stumbled towards a tree to hold onto. I saw Omar kneeling and rubbing his forehead. I closed my eyes and just breathed.

Seeing a sharp, unforgiving branch impaling Veronica's neck was equal parts gruesome and devastating. Veronica's lifeless body traumatized me.

It didn't seem real. How were Henry and Veronica both dead? It was something that was never supposed to happen. It was fate playing it's cruel hand twice. When I opened my eyes, Omar sauntered towards me with a paper note in his hand, he silently handed it to me.

"*My entire life has been a lie. At least now I'll be with my Henry,*" I whispered to myself.

"Suicide note," Omar said softly.

"Oh god," I gasped.

"It's over," Omar grimaced.

I heard voices and footsteps stomping on soaked leaves in the ground. The search unit.

"Aw shit," Omar quickly turned and ran forward.

It was too late. He had already seen the body. Everyone had. Felix slowly trudged up to her and briefly held out his hand. I couldn't tell if he had tears in his eyes or if it was the torrential rain that was pouring down on all of us. He stared at the grisly image of her death as the police set up a perimeter with yellow tape. He walked away by himself and sat down on a nearby rock. Judging by his sorrowful expression, he was beyond devastated.

It was all over the local news within the hour. *Veronica Cain, mother of slain Skyview Falls student and star athlete, Henry Cain, was found dead after missing for two consecutive days. Cause of death is suspected to be ruled as a suicide.*

There was about ten different variations of that bombshell headline and every time I read it, I still couldn't believe it. Veronica Cain was dead. My former best friend. She was gone forever. I couldn't even imagine what Lawrence was going through. He lost his beloved son and wife in less than a month. He had all the money in the world and no amount could bring back the people he loved most. After I dried up, I had a coffee with Willow to speak about the recent tragedy. There wasn't much to say except that it was shocking and unexpected. That year was the most tragic one ever in Skyview Falls. When I came home I caught Ethan on the way out. He was wearing his old basketball uniform.

"Where are you going?" I asked.

"I'm going to shoot around. It's been a while. I miss it," Ethan said.

"That's good. Can we talk first? Please?" I asked.

Ethan sighed and plopped down on the couch.

"What's up mom?" Ethan asked.

"How are you doing?" I asked.

"I'm good," Ethan said.

"I assume that you heard about what happened to Henry's mother," I said.

"Yeah, it's insane. I can't believe she'd do that to herself."

"I didn't expect it either. I don't think anyone did," I said.

"Do you think she was really sad about Henry?" Ethan asked.

"I think she was, honey," I said.

"They're both dead. That's crazy," Ethan muttered.

"Ethan, I have to ask. Will you ever forgive me?"

"Look, mom, I love you, but you hurt me. Just give me some time, okay? All this horrible news about murder and death has really got me down. I need to clear my head. Is that alright?" Ethan asked.

"Of course," I replied.

He came over, gave me a tight hug then rushed out. I couldn't help but smile. Maybe I had been overthinking the whole time. I did raise my son right and I did not teach him to be a murderer. He was innocent. He always was. I didn't know who Henry's murderer was, but it wasn't Ethan. A consolation in the wake of Veronica's tragic death. I thought about Veronica's suicide note.

My entire life has been a lie. At least now I'll be with my Henry.

I figured that she meant her life with Lawrence was a lie since she married him for his riches, or it could've meant that her life without Henry was a lie. Whatever it was and despite everything she did to me, I hoped she was at peace. My phone rang. It was Felix. I had no idea what to expect after he was broken into a million pieces because of Veronica's death. I answered it and held my breath.

"*Hey Sonya,*" Felix said.

"*Hi Felix.*"

"*The police have asked to talk to me again regarding Henry's murder case.*" Felix said.

"*Okay. Is something wrong?*" I asked.

"*Sonya, I'm going to confess and tell the truth,*" Felix said.

"*What? What are you talking about?*" I asked.

My heart began to race so fast, it felt like it was tearing a hole through my chest.

"*It's all my fault. I murdered Henry. Henry found out about something he shouldn't have,*" Felix confessed.

"*Felix, are you serious? You killed him?*" I asked, my voice shaking.

"*I'm sorry for cheating on you. I'm sorry for making you suffer. I'm sorry about not being a better dad to the kids. It's all over now, Sonya. I know you'll take care of Ethan and Santi. You always have,*" Felix stated.

"*Felix, what the hell is this? You can't just drop something like this over the phone. Seriously, what the hell is going on?*" I asked.

"*My life is a lie, Sonya. All I've done is lie.*"

"*Why Felix? Why? Why did you kill him? Explain yourself,*" I urged.

"*You'll know the truth. Veronica knew too.*"

"*What truth? What are you talking about? Answer me!*"

He hung up. I couldn't accept that from him. I couldn't trust the mental state he was in after Veronica's suicide. It was obvious that he had been in love with her since the day they met. It didn't matter anymore. All I wanted was the truth, in order to prove my son's innocence once and for all.

I rushed to Felix's house and saw a lively scene. Blue and red lights flashed everywhere as I counted 6 police cruisers parked in Felix's driveway. He was outside in handcuffs. Omar was speaking with him. I parked on the street and ran out. Several police officers yelled at me to get back so I did while raising my hand so Omar would see. When he spotted me, he jogged over.

"What's going on, Omar?" I asked.

"I can't say much right now but it's over, Sonya. It's over. We got him," Omar said.

"I understand."

"Felix is Henry's killer," Omar mouthed.

It was over just like that. Felix had confessed to Henry's murder and had been arrested. He had been the true killer all along. The only thing that remained was why? Why did Felix murder Henry? What lies was Felix talking about? I found out soon enough.

CHAPTER 20

Felix's arrest hadn't been publicized yet as the police department knew it would rock the town to its core. They needed to brace themselves for the impact and get their ducks in a row. In the midst of that chaos, I received an unexpected phone call from Lawrence. I thought he was gonna invite me to Veronica's funeral.

He didn't, but he did want to meet somewhere secluded. He had urgent information to share with me. Information that was highly secretive. It freaked me out a bit, but I went along with it. We met in an abandoned warehouse district. I parked in between two empty shipping containers. He came out from behind and calmly walked towards my car. He quietly climbed in and stared forward.

"Hi Lawrence," I said.

"Hey Sonya."

"I know we talked about it over the phone but I'm really sorry about Veronica. I wished things didn't pan out this way," I said.

"I'm sorry too. I saw it coming but I couldn't do anything to stop it. I'll live with that for the rest of my life."

"At least she's with Henry now."

"That's one silver lining," Lawrence scoffed.

"So, why the secrecy? We're in an abandoned warehouse lot and you look very anxious. What's going on?" I asked.

"After we talked at the coffee shop, I finally mustered up the courage to clean out Henry's bedroom. I hadn't stepped foot in there since his death. I wanted to learn about who my son really was. Sonya, it was the biggest mistake of my life," Lawrence said.

"Jesus, Lawrence. What did you find?" I asked.

What immediately came to mind was something similar to what was on Mr. Griffin's computer files. I sincerely hoped he wasn't involved in those deplorable, pedophilic chat rooms and forums. If Lawrence found any illegal pictures and told Veronica, it would've explained her state of mind and why she went off the deep end.

"There was something hidden, beneath his bed frame," Lawrence said.

"What was it? Pictures?" I asked.

"No, it was an official document of a DNA test," Lawrence said.

"A DNA test?" I asked.

"This is going to be very difficult to hear, but it's the truth and Veronica confessed it all. The DNA test proves it," Lawrence said.

"You're scaring me, Lawrence."

He swallowed hard and pulled out a document. It was a DNA test. As I read it over, it felt like a fist enveloped with fire was pushing through my chest and yanking out my heart.

"This says that Felix is Henry's father."

My chest tightened and I had trouble breathing for several seconds. I silently calmed myself down as I gripped my seat.

"That's right. I'm not his father. I haven't been his father this whole time," Lawrence revealed.

"Holy shit. This is insanity," I voiced.

"In that short span of time that Felix and Veronica dated, Felix got Veronica pregnant. I don't think he ever knew or maybe he secretly did. I don't know," Lawrence said.

"She kept it a secret this whole time," I whispered.

I was beyond furious. I couldn't believe it. My entire marriage was built on secrets and lies. My friendship with Veronica was the same. What was real? What was a lie? I couldn't tell anymore. It made me violently sick to my stomach. I could only imagine how Lawrence felt. He cared for, loved, and mourned a child that wasn't his.

"She lied to me about being pregnant with my child. Henry wasn't my son. He never was," Lawrence stated.

"She wanted your money that badly. That's despicable," I derided.

"I would've never guessed that Henry wasn't my biological son. My entire life with Veronica and Henry was a lie," Lawrence said.

"My god, Lawrence. I'm really sorry."

"It's alright. My life is in shambles but I'm trying to hang on," Lawrence uttered.

"I think Felix murdered Henry because Henry learned the secret. He found out that Felix was his dad and threatened to tell everyone. He may have even revealed it to Felix for the first time. He dug his own grave without realizing it."

"I think that's plausible. I just don't understand why Henry would request a DNA test in the first place."

"Maybe he had a gut feeling. Maybe deep down he knew," I theorized.

"I suppose we'll never truly know," Lawrence sighed.

"I'm as angry as you are. This is absolutely devastating," I said.

"After she confessed everything to me, I wanted to devote my life to destroying hers. Before I could say or do anything, she left. You know what happened next. I let it happen, Sonya. I was so angry I let her destroy herself. I never wanted to see her again. I got my wish," Lawrence said.

"She kept a horrible secret from you. She allowed you to live a lie for over 16 years," I replied softly.

"My family is now nothing because of Veronica's lies. Henry was never my son, and his real father murdered him because of a secret that should've never been revealed."

One dark secret. That's what it took to rip two families apart and to shock the entire town. If the secret remained buried, nothing would've happened at all. Henry inadvertently caused his own murder and set in motion a series of events that changed all of our lives forever.

Felix was Henry's father. I thought. A shocking, explosive revelation with disastrous consequences for us all. The only consolation I had was that Ethan was innocent. My job was completed. The only thing I could do then was wait for news about Felix's arrest.

CHAPTER 21

I sat across Ethan and Santi in my home as I delivered the news about Felix, their father. I didn't dare tell them anything else. They didn't need to know.

"Alright boys, I'm going to tell you something that's going to be very hard to hear," I sighed.

"What happened mom?" Santi asked.

Ethan remained quiet and looked down.

"Your father has been arrested," I said softly.

"What? Why?" Ethan asked.

"He's a cop. How would he get arrested?" Santi asked.

"There's no easy way to say this but he confessed to murdering Henry. He was the one all along. He was Henry's killer," I revealed.

They both stared at me with shocked, frightened eyes. I could sense all of their confusion, bewilderment, anger, and anxiousness all at once.

"Are you serious?" Santi asked.

"I am. I'm sorry. It's been very hard for me too., I was married to him after all," I said.

"Dad killed someone. That's insane, mom. That means he's the guy who slashed Henry's throat," Santi gasped.

"That does mean that, yes," I whispered.

"How could he ever do something like that? Why would he? What did Henry do to him?" Santi asked.

"Those are questions we don't know the answers to yet. The police are still investigating," I said.

"This means dad's going to jail, doesn't it?" Santi asked.

"He will most likely be given a jail sentence."

"Holy shit, man. Our dad is really a murderer. That's fucked up," Ethan expressed.

"I know it is. So if you guys want to talk about it, I'm here. We'll get through it together."

I stood up and went around to hug them.

"So this means we're not visiting dad anymore?" Santi asked.

"That's correct," I said.

"So everything changes," Ethan uttered.

"It does. I hope you guys don't mind staying with me all the time," I said.

"Not at all," Santi said.

"I don't mind," Ethan said with a small smile.

He seemed to be warming up to me again which made my heart full. Things were very tough, but they finally seemed to be looking up.

"The good news is, no one will question Ethan's innocence ever again after they announce Felix's arrest," I said.

"It's about damn time," Ethan mumbled.

"Now instead of the kids bullying me about Ethan, they're gonna bully me about dad," Santi said.

"No they won't. We won't let them. I promise. We'll end it together," Ethan said holding out his hand. Santi clasped it and they nodded at each other. That's what I loved to see. My two boys looking out for each other and protecting one another. Omar called so I went into another room and answered.

"*What's up?*" I asked.

"*Sonya, turn on your TV in half an hour. Chief Delatorre is holding a press conference regarding Felix's arrest,*" Omar said.

"*So it's official then, huh?*" I asked.

"*We got the evidence we needed. Delatorre is desperate to close this case and we'll be doing that today. I'm sorry, Sonya. I know he's your ex-husband and the father of your kids and all. He was my friend once too.*"

"*It's been a real shock, but it might end up being for the better, you know? Obviously it's terrible he turned out to be the killer, but Henry's murderer needed to be brought to justice.*" I said.

"*The whole department is absolutely appalled that he did it. I can't believe it either to be honest. He wasn't the best cop, but I didn't think he was a killer.*"

"*I guess the signs were there all along. I chose to ignore them,*" I said.

"*All that matters is that it's over, Sonya. It's finally over. This case was driving everyone mad, including you and Ethan.*"

"*I feel like I can finally breathe again. Ethan's innocent and no one will dare take that away from him again.*"

"I'm happy for you two."

"Thank you, Omar. You've been insanely helpful throughout this entire thing. I could always count on you. Seriously, I owe you."

"No worries, Sonya. I'm happy to help," Omar said.

"I'll talk to you soon," I said as I hung up.

It was high time I started moving on from Felix. I didn't want to feel sorry for myself anymore. I turned on the TV a half hour later and saw Chief Delatorre gearing up to address a panel of local news reporters and journalists. They were all in a white conference room. Everyone was sitting down, while Chief Delatorre stood behind a podium with a microphone. Omar, Stanley, and a few other officers stood on opposite sides of him.

"Good afternoon everyone. Right off the bat I want to say, yes, the rumors are true. Felix Salvador has been arrested in connection with the Henry Cain murder case and we will be prosecuting. We have uncovered outstanding evidence that pinpoints Felix Salvador as Henry's murderer beyond a reasonable doubt. This police department is shocked, and saddened at this revelation. We held Felix in high esteem as a police officer and felt he did great work. He was responsible, passionate, and committed to safeguarding this community. He has shattered that solemn vow and has betrayed this community. We only hope that this was an isolated case, and that this department won't make a habit of producing secret criminals and killers. I'll be personally monitoring things more closely and will strive to ensure this department is clean. Thank you. I'll answer a few questions now."

The reporters and journalists clamored to get Chief Delatorre's attention as one question was on everyone's minds. Why did Felix murder Henry Cain? I turned off the TV and went to check on Ethan. I found him getting ready to go to sleep. I sat on the edge of his bed and waited for him to tuck himself in.

"Are you doing okay, Ethan? Do you wanna talk about anything?"

"Yeah, I'm good. Thanks, mom."

"Okay, sweetheart. I love you."

"I love you too."

When I was about to stand up, Ethan grabbed my hand. Concern was washed all over his face. I grew nervous.

"What's wrong, honey?"

"Do you mean that? Do you really love me?"

"Of course I do, Ethan. You're my son and I'm proud of you."

"Mom, I have to tell you something."

I had been anticipating this. I knew that deep down Ethan knew more than what he let on about Henry's murder. I didn't know why he was keeping it a secret, but I figured that he must've had his reasons.

"You already knew your dad killed Henry, didn't you?"

"No, mom. I'm the one who killed Henry."

I killed Henry. It hit me like an 800-pound bull charging full speed ahead at me, goring me with its horns. I remained motionless and my mind went blank for what seemed like hours as I attempted to process what Ethan had just said. He couldn't have killed him. It simply wasn't possible. Ethan wasn't a murderer. He was just a boy. Felix was Henry's murderer, end of story.

"No. No you didn't."

"Mom, I did," Ethan's voice trembled.

"No."

"Mom, I did."

"Be quiet."

"What?"

"Stop talking that nonsense. You are not a killer, Ethan. You would never do it. Why are you saying that?"

"I'm so sorry, mom. I'm so sorry. I messed up. I messed up big time." Ethan sobbed.

"You didn't do anything, Ethan. You're making it up. Felix did it."

"I should've been asking for your forgiveness this whole time."

I leaned and softly caressed his head while tears rolled down my cheeks. I felt excruciating pain at the pit of my stomach that was shutting down my entire body. I had no idea what to say. I had no idea what to do.

"Ethan, I don't believe you. I don't believe that you killed your best friend."

"It was the last night I showed up late to the house."

"Ethan don't go there, don't tell me that."

Ethan slowly stood up and walked over to his dresser. He pulled out the very last drawer and dug his hands all the way at the bottom. He pulled out a shirt. It was a varsity warm-up. It had bloodied stains all over it. He held it up for me to see. I gasped and put my hand to my mouth. I had to stop myself from screaming. I didn't need to freak out Santi.

"This is the shirt I was wearing when I murdered Henry."

I stayed quiet for several seconds. I slowly breathed in, and out before I spiraled into a full-blown panic attack.

"Ethan, what happened?" I croaked.

This was the whole story as he remembered it. They had met up that fateful night in the Blackwood Forest after basketball practice. Ethan had asked him to speak alone. Nobody else knew what was happening between them. He made sure to keep it a secret. He had kept the box cutter from Mr. Griffin because he had planned to use it against Henry. As they walked together deeper, and deeper into the forest, Henry grew antsy and wanted answers.

"Yo bro, what's going on? You've been quiet. What did you need to tell me?" Henry asked.

"Let's stop walking," Ethan suggested.

They stopped in the middle of a densely shaded area near a ravine. That detail was familiar.

"Okay. What's up?" Henry asked.

"I need to talk to you about something very important," Ethan urged.

"I'm listening, dude. I don't know why you're dragging this out so much. I want to go home," Henry whined.

"What have you been doing to Layla?" Ethan asked.

Henry laughed and shook his head.

"Oh no, not this. I haven't done anything to her. We don't need to talk about this," Henry brushed him off.

"That's not true. Don't bullshit me, Henry. We are going to talk about this. You're not gonna shrug me off," Ethan demanded.

"Dude, I didn't do anything to her. I swear," Henry pleaded.

"I know you've been touching her," Ethan hissed.

"It's all jokes, man. You know how I am. I like to have fun. I tease her," Henry said.

"Yeah? You like to have fun? Feeling up a girl's ass without permission is fun to you? What the fuck is wrong with you?" Ethan asked.

"Alright, time out. Let's back track. Who the *fuck* said I was doing that?" Henry asked.

"A lot of people that we know have told me what you're doing," Ethan said.

"Who? Who the hell is snitching? I'll get 'em straight," Henry threatened.

"I'm not telling you shit," Ethan growled.

"Look, I don't really appreciate you accusing me of doing something I'm not doing. That's not cool bro. We're supposed to be friends, we're supposed to be *brothers*!" Henry exclaimed.

Ethan took out the box cutter, and slowly approached Henry.

"I'm not here to play games, Henry. I want you to stay the hell away from Layla. If I hear that you're bothering her or any girl again, you're done for. That means Beth too. She's the principal's daughter. What the hell were you thinking?! I swear I'll fuck you up. Do you understand me?" Ethan held up the knife towards him.

"You're not doing anything to me, you fucking psycho. I haven't done anything bad. Why are you threatening me?" Henry asked.

"Why? Because you're being sexual with *my* girlfriend. I don't want you going near her ever again. If you do, we're gonna have some serious problems," Ethan said.

"Dude, put that knife away. You're not gonna do anything to me, you're acting like a psycho." Henry laughed.

"Yeah? You wanna try me?" Ethan asked.

"You're behaving like a fucking freak!" Henry shouted.

"You're behaving like Griffin," Ethan snapped back.

There was a loud silence as Henry's face twisted with rage.

"Don't you dare bring him up. I'm *nothing* like him. You're out of your mind!" Henry roared.

"You're going down that path, Henry," Ethan mocked.

"You don't know the things he's done to me. You don't know what he is. You're crossing a line," Henry thundered.

"You crossed the line the minute you touched your best friend's girlfriend!" Ethan bellowed.

"She never said she didn't like it," Henry teased.

"What the hell did you just say?!" Ethan yelled as he inched forward. Henry took a step back.

"You're really pissing me off, Ethan. You need to step back, before you get hurt," Henry warned.

"I don't care. You're behaving like trash. Don't get mad because I'm calling you out on it, you fucking *pervert*," Ethan spat.

Henry giggled, and started clapping his hands.

"Oh I get what this is," Henry smiled.

"What?"

"You're jealous of me." Henry smirked.

"What the hell are you talking about?" Ethan said.

"You're jealous I'm a better basketball player than you, and that I can steal Layla from you whenever I want. I can have Beth too, I own the damn school. I don't give a shit about Jacobson," Henry mocked.

"You're insane. I'm not jealous of you," Ethan snapped.

"You know what's worst of all?" Henry asked.

"What, you idiot?" Ethan asked.

"You're jealous your own father loves me more than you," Henry proclaimed.

That painfully stung Ethan. Ethan felt a need to impress him during the basketball games, but typically cracked under the pressure. He didn't know how to get his own father to love him.

"You don't know what the hell you're talking about," Ethan stated.

"I wasn't gonna do this yet, but screw it. It's high time you accepted the truth," Henry said as he set down his bag, and sifted through the front zipper. He pulled out an official document, and slowly treaded towards Ethan to show him. Ethan let his guard down.

"What is that?" Ethan asked.

"A DNA test," Henry answered.

"Of what?" Ethan asked.

"Look at it, Ethan" Henry replied.

Ethan took a few steps forward, and studied it. He jumped back, and dropped the box cutter.

"What the hell? That can't be real. That's fake!" Ethan shouted.

"It's real. Felix is my dad. He's been my real dad all along," Henry revealed.

"No. That doesn't make any sense. That would mean that my dad and your mom—," Ethan trailed.

"I'm sorry, Ethan," Henry said softly.

"You were never Lawrence's son," Ethan whispered.

"It happened sixteen years ago, Ethan. I've been living a lie for sixteen years, but now I know the truth. Now, you know it too," Henry proudly stated.

"I don't know what to say," Ethan replied.

"I told you, Ethan. *Brothers for life*. I was right all along," Henry placed a fist on his chest.

"You're my brother," Ethan gasped.

"I always wondered why Felix gave me so much attention. I thought he was just a huge basketball fan. It turns out it was a lot more than that," Henry said.

"Why the hell would you even do that test?" Ethan asked.

"I found an old picture of Felix with my mom in college. They seemed cozy so I really thought about it. My parents barely show any affection towards each other. It became obvious to me, but I needed to confirm it and I did," Henry confessed.

"This is fucking nuts. I can't believe this," Ethan mumbled.

"I'm sorry that I'm the better son, Ethan," Henry claimed.

"You're not better than me, you egomaniac," Ethan snapped.

"I am. Our father loves me more than he loves you," Henry mocked.

Ethan collapsed to the ground, and started crying. He couldn't believe it. Henry was his half-brother all along. Everything made sense to him. Their father gave Henry more love, and attention because he was the better player. He was bigger and stronger. He played better in clutch situations, he was a vocal leader, and he was the most likely to play college basketball. He was the better son.

"I hate you. I fucking hate you, Henry," Ethan blubbered.

Henry slowly walked over to Ethan, and crouched down. He put his hand on his shoulder.

"Hey man, just because that's the truth doesn't mean he doesn't love you too. Remember, we're brothers and we're in this together." Henry comforted him.

"Together?" Ethan asked.

"What are the odds that we've been related all along? We've been best friends forever, and now we find out that we're actually brothers connected by blood. We're meant to look after each other forever, Ethan," Henry voiced.

"I guess so," Ethan grumbled.

"I have to tell you the truth about Layla," Henry whispered.

"What truth?" Ethan asked.

"She's no good for you, Ethan. She's a whore. She's a complete whore who craves attention from guys," Henry urged.

Ethan's ears started ringing as he felt a volcanic surge of rage expand through his stomach.

"What?" Ethan asked.

"She likes being touched by other men. She practically begs for it, dude. She's like Beth. She is a complete *slut*. I wouldn't lie to you. You're my brother after all," Henry said.

"Layla is my girlfriend, and I love her. Why are you saying that shit? What the hell is wrong with you?" Ethan asked.

"Ethan, it's the truth. You have to break up with her. She'll drive us apart," Henry demanded.

"No. You know what the truth is? You've torn me down for a very long time. You always said you were better than me at everything, and I believed you. I let myself down so you could bring yourself up. The teams, the coaches, and even our own father liked you better than me. I hate you, Henry. I've secretly hated you my entire life," Ethan confessed.

Ethan slowly looked down at the box cutter on the ground. Henry met his eyes with a mixed expression of confusion, and dread.

"Ethan. Don't do it," Henry warned.

Ethan lunged forward, scooped up the box cutter, unsheathed the sharp blade and tackled Henry to the ground, pinning him down.

"No! Don't do it! No, no, no, no! Please! I have a future! We have a future, Ethan!" Henry begged.

Ethan was in a state of blind fury, and turned into an ultra-violent beast as he repeatedly stabbed, and slashed Henry's throat. As the blood gushed out of the multiple wounds in his neck, Henry silently pleaded *why* over and over again. Once it was clear that Henry was almost dead, Ethan remained on top of him and caught his breath.

"You piece of shit. I've always hated you. You always thought you were better than me. Not anymore. You're done. You're fucking done. Your life is over. Burn in hell," Ethan roared.

Henry desperately sucked in escaping breaths, and sputtered out blood. He hastily tried to keep in the blood that was spilling out of his split-open throat, with his trembling hands.

As a final blow, Ethan told me he got up, and dragged Henry's half-dead body near a hillside. He struggled mightily, but managed to push him over. Henry let out a blood-gurgling shriek as he dropped fast, and hard. He violently landed on his back, on top of a large jagged rock near a flowing ravine. *Crunch*. Henry's spine shattered instantly as his shocked eyes rolled back, and his jaw went slack.

Ethan peeked over, and saw his dead body. At first Ethan smirked, satisfied with Henry's death. But then reality set in, and a hundred thoughts stormed his mind all at once. The raging guilt broiled in Ethan's stomach causing him to violently puke into the river. After several seconds, Ethan climbed down the hill to vigorously clean off Henry's blood from his hands in the water. He took Henry's phone and smashed it to pieces with his foot. Ethan then took one long gaze at Henry's lifeless body.

"Sorry, *brother*," Ethan whispered.

He sprinted away, and left him to rot. Ethan charged through the forest like a frightened animal. His legs burned with agonizing pain, and the air tore through his lungs like icicles. Sheer adrenaline surged through Ethan's veins as he tried to escape the most horrific crime he had ever committed. Ethan glanced down, and saw that his varsity warm-up shirt was filled with Henry's blood. He quickly pulled it off. He needed to hide it quickly. That bloodied piece of evidence along with the bloodied knife would lead the murder back to him. Ethan had no intention of ever being caught.

When he finished telling the story, to say that I was shocked was a severe understatement. I remained quiet for a long time. I was never going to see my son the same way again. The way he described stabbing, and slashing Henry's throat was the most gruesome, vicious thing I had ever heard.

The fact that he also dragged his half-dead body while he was choking on his own blood was horrifying. I also couldn't believe that he threw him off a hill onto a rock that shattered his spine. I didn't understand what I had heard. I didn't understand why a malicious, cruel force possessed my son to murder Henry the way he did. I really didn't know who my son was after all. He had committed the ghastliest crime in the history of Skyview Falls.

Despite all that and despite everything, he was still my son at the end of the day. Even though I would never see him the same way again, I still loved him. I would be his mother until the end of time. I held him in my belly for 9 months and gave birth to him. I held him in my arms when he was the size of a peanut. I watched him grow, and change into a mature, young man before my very eyes. I would never hate him, and I would never judge him. I would protect him forever. I chose Ethan over Henry, and over everyone else.

I tightly hugged Ethan as he whimpered in my arms.

"I'm a monster, mom. I'm a killer. What am I going to do?"

"You are never ever going to repeat that story for as long as you live," I demanded.

"Are you sure? Dad took the fall. I don't know what to do," Ethan whispered.

"Wait, your dad told you something?" I asked.

"He called me before he turned himself in. He told me he always had a feeling that Henry was his, but never said anything because he was afraid of what it would do to your marriage," Ethan revealed.

"Our relationship was doomed to fail from the start then. Do you know why he confessed to Henry's murder?" I asked.

"He told me he failed one son; he didn't want to fail another. I think he knew deep down that I did it. I never told him, but I think he knew," Ethan admitted.

Felix always seemed to believe that Ethan was the killer. I hated him more for it, but he turned out to be right. At least he was finally doing something that proved he did love Ethan after all.

"Let him take the fall, Ethan. He owes it to you. Do you understand me? He owes it to you, and to us. We won't let what you did destroy our family, and our lives. We will be ruined forever if it's revealed that you murdered him. You tell no one, not even Santi. You never ever say a word of this to anybody. You pretend it never happened. Am I clear?" I asked.

Ethan furiously nodded.

"Okay, mom. I won't say anything. I promise. I don't wanna go to prison. I don't want my life to be ruined. I still want to see you,

Santi, and Layla whenever I want. My life can't go to shit now. I'm too young, right?"

"Do as I say, and nothing will ever happen to you. When we carefully get rid of that shirt, it'll be over with. Do you have anything else that might incriminate you?" I asked.

"I kept the DNA test he had."

"We'll shred it, and burn it. Anything else?"

"I already destroyed his phone."

"Good. Does Layla know about any of this?"

"No. When I went to her house I made up an excuse. I said I went on a run after practice. Truth is, I needed my duffel bag to hide the evidence."

"That's fine, keep it that way. Do not tell Layla. I know you love her, but we don't know how she would react. It could blow everything up."

"Is it bad if I tried to frame Mr. Griffin for the murder?" Ethan asked.

"Jesus, Ethan. You put the bloodied box cutter in his classroom?" I asked.

"It was me. I figured that if the police saw him with that, he was done for. I was willing to try anything to get away with murder. I'm a monster. I'm a horrible person."

"We'll be just fine, Ethan. I promise you. I will protect you."

"Mom, do you hate me? Do you hate me because I'm a monster? I killed someone. I got a knife, and stabbed him in the throat so many times. The blood was everywhere. He was screaming but you couldn't even hear it because the blood was filling his mouth. I'm evil, mom. I murdered my best friend like a bloodthirsty animal. Why did Henry have to say all that stuff about Layla? Why did he have to touch her at all? What the fuck is wrong with him? What the fuck is wrong with me?" Ethan buried his face in his hands.

"Hey, listen to me. You are a good boy. Okay? You are good. We are gonna live our lives, and be normal. That is it. Okay? I love you, Ethan. I'll never stop loving you," I said as I kissed the top of his head.

"I love you too, mom."

We all lie to save ourselves, and we must do it now.

That night I decided to embrace that wholeheartedly. I decided to live a good, happy life with my children. Henry's death was an unspeakable tragedy that drove his mother Veronica Cain to suicide, and it ripped apart the Cain family forever. But, as far as anyone knew, Ethan was innocent, and he would remain innocent forever.

We both had that in common now. My son was a murderer, but so was I.

EPILOGUE
A FEW MONTHS LATER

Felix wore a bright orange jumpsuit while he fiddled with a deck of playing cards in his cell block. He sat on one of the benches and continued to work on an object he was making. There weren't that many prison guards around. Most of the trouble brewed in other sectors. Felix knew this. He glanced up and saw the back of a man's head. It was someone he recognized. Someone he knew. Felix's heart began beating like a drum as he stood and strolled towards him. He tried his best to keep his cool so the guards wouldn't deem him suspicious.

When he reached the man, he tapped him on the shoulder. The man flinched and turned around, fearing for his life.

"Hello."

"Hey, Mr. Griffin," Felix said.

"No one has called me that in a very long time," Mr. Griffin replied.

"You just transferred here?" Felix asked.

"I did. There was a lot of issues in the other facility. I feared for my safety," Mr. Griffin said.

"Cool, I get it man. Do you wanna play cards?" Felix asked.

"Okay, sure. That's harmless enough," Mr. Griffin agreed.

"Alright, you get to pick your first card. Go right in the middle," Felix said.

Mr. Griffin reached into the middle and pulled out a card. He noticed a toothbrush was taped to it.

"This is odd storage for a toothbrush," Mr. Griffin wondered aloud.

"That one isn't finished yet. This one is," Felix scattered the cards in Mr. Griffin's face and tackled him to the floor.

He took out a sharpened shiv made from the bottom of a toothbrush, and ferociously stabbed Mr. Griffin to death. He began at the stomach and made his way up to his neck. Mr. Griffin screamed in utter agony as dozens of dark red holes spilled out all over his body. When Felix got to his neck, Mr. Griffin coughed up so much blood it spilled onto the floor, creating a huge dark pool of thick red liquid. The horrified prison guards called for an emergency lockdown, and rushed towards Felix to stop the massacre. It was far too late. Felix had ended his life in under a minute.

"I know I'm a huge piece of shit, but you're a whole different breed. Your life should've ended a long time ago," Felix snarled.

Prison had made Felix bitter and vengeful. He had been forced to become an animal of violence to survive. One task he wanted to achieve was to butcher Mr. Griffin alive if ever given the chance for what he did to Ethan, Henry and so many other kids. He knew his life was over, but he didn't care. Mr. Griffin was gone and after losing so much, that's all that mattered to Felix.

Ethan was called down to Principal Jacobson's office, after being reported by a teacher for displaying affection with his girlfriend, Layla.

"Just make sure it doesn't happen again, okay? Or, you know— do it when no one's looking. I don't care," Willow said.

"I got you. Thank you."

"Anytime."

"Can I ask you a question?" Ethan asked, a lump forming in his throat.

"Sure thing."

"Do you— do you think we did the right thing?"

"Of course we did," Willow whispered.

"Why do I still feel so guilty? I lied to my mom too. I never told her about you. I never told her we discussed it."

"You know you can't," Willow said sternly.

"I know."

"Look, Henry had it coming. He abused my only daughter, Beth. He *raped* her, Ethan. He needed to pay for that. Remember, you came to me. You told me what was happening. If you didn't go through with it, I would've."

"I know," Ethan said softly.

"It's over, Ethan. No need to bring up the past."

"You pushed him over the hill. You watched as his spine broke in half."

"I did."

"It needed to be done."

"Exactly," Willow stated.

"We all lie to save ourselves, huh?" Ethan asked.

"If we have to."

"I'll see you around." Ethan grimaced and left.

Willow had convinced Ethan to murder Henry, after he told her what he had done to Beth, her daughter. Willow followed Ethan and Henry, after Ethan told her when he planned to do it. She was there to ensure it would be done. She promised he would get away with it. She had been the one to push Henry over, to make sure he was dead and gone.

Ethan exited the office and took out his phone. It had been recording audio. He stopped it, and opened his messages.

> I got it.

> OMAR: Are you sure you want to go through with this? I promised your mother I would protect you.

> I came to you and confessed because I was tired of the lies. I don't need protect myself anymore. I need to tell the truth.

> OMAR: Your life will be over, Ethan. I can promise you that. Your mother, Santi, your friends…you'll never see them again. You'll never play high school basketball again, and you'll never get a chance to play college basketball. Last chance to forget this ever happened.

> I'm done with the lies. I'm done lying to save myself.

Like father, like son.

THE END.

THANK YOU READER!

Thank you so much for reading *MY SON IS A MURDERER*! If you loved this book, be sure to stay subscribed to my newsletter for free books, updates about future books and more!

Sign up at spencerguerreroauthor.com!

PLEASE REVIEW!

Please do not forget to leave a review on Amazon, Goodreads, and other social media platforms! Your reviews are always read by me and greatly appreciated!

You can follow me on Instagram, Facebook, Goodreads and Amazon!

Instagram: @spencergauthor

Facebook: @Spencer Guerrero – Author

MORE BOOKS AVAILABLE!

Please consider leaving a review! I read them all! It helps me immensely as an author!

I have FOUR other standalone psychological mystery-thriller novels OUT NOW!

MY FATHER IS A SERIAL KILLER, *MY WIFE'S STALKER*, *A MURDER IN THE NEIGHBORHOOD* and *MY MOTHER-IN-LAW MUST DIE!*

They're available in paperback/digital formats on Amazon and on Kindle Unlimited!

DEDICATION

I want to give a huge shout out and thanks for my family for supporting me and encouraging me throughout my long journey of wanting to be a writer and an author. Mom, Dad, Sebastian, and Sophia. There has been a lot of ups and downs. There were even times where I wanted to give up and was frustrated beyond understanding. You could've easily shot down my dreams and tell me that I would never make it. That has never been the case and I'm very lucky for that. I love you guys and I appreciate you!

I also wanted to give a huge thanks to my childhood best friends for always supporting me and giving me words of encouragement throughout this journey. Enrique, Berto, Mike, Cesar, Eric. I've known you guys for over 14 years, and I hope we remain friends forever. Cheers to more laughs and goofing off with you guys.

A huge thank you to my good friend Laura as well. I love being able to talk about writing and books with you. I'll always appreciate your friendship and support!

There are a lot of other people who have in one way or another, have given me words of encouragement and support in other ways. Please know that I appreciate you all! You keep me going.

To my readers, you are the lifeline. You are the reason I write books. You are the reason why I'm so passionate to get these stories out there. I'm very lucky to have you all. I read and appreciate every single review beyond measure. I love books so much and I love being able to share mine with you all!

A HUGE thank you to the readers/authors of the Facebook Groups: Psychological Thriller Readers and the BookLounge!! You have boosted the attention for this book by so much! Appreciate you all! Now…let me release the breath I didn't realize I was holding…

ABOUT THE AUTHOR

My name is Spencer Guerrero. I was born and raised in Florida, and I am of Nicaraguan descent. I am a self-published author and writer of domestic/psychological mystery-thrillers and suspense-thrillers.

I used to be a freelance screenwriter and was hired to write a religious sci-fi/fantasy book adaptation, an animated Christmas film script, three short films and other work that included writing and outlining stories for licensed animated characters.

I decided to switch avenues so I could focus on the type of stories I wanted to write. Self-publishing looked like the best route, and I haven't looked back since.

My favorite genres are YA fiction, mystery-thriller, fantasy, and literary fiction. Other than that, I like funny cat memes, dark comedies and I play basketball!

Printed in Great Britain
by Amazon